Nancy Drew
in
The Quest of the Missing Map

This Armada book belongs to:

A S

The Nancy Drew Mystery Stories

The Quest of the Missing Map

Carolyn Keene

Armada

First published in the U.K. in 1971 by
William Collins Sons & Co. Ltd., London and Glasgow.
First published in Armada in 1973 by
Fontana Paperbacks,
14 St. James's Place, London SW1A 1PS.

This impression 1981

Printed in Great Britain by
Love & Malcomson Ltd., Brighton Road,
Redhill, Surrey.

CONTENTS

"Leave here at once and never come back!"
the stranger warned

·1·

The Haunted House

HER golden-red hair flying in the wind, Nancy Drew ran up the porch steps and opened the front door of her home.

She could hear Hannah Gruen, the Drews' housekeeper, saying to someone in the living-room, "Why don't you tell your mysterious story to Nancy? She's a really clever young detective."

The mere mention of a mystery quickened the pulse of eighteen-year-old Nancy. She dropped her art books and portfolio on the hall table and glanced into the living-room.

"Come in, dear," said Mrs Gruen. "You're home early."

"Art school was dismissed at two-thirty today," Nancy replied.

Seated on a couch beside Mrs Gruen was an attractive, dark-haired girl about twenty.

"Nancy, I'd like you to meet Ellen Smith," the middle-aged, kindly housekeeper said. "You've frequently heard me speak of her."

The girls greeted each other, then Ellen said, "I was hoping Mrs Gruen might go with me to Rocky Edge this afternoon. I just dread going alone." She glanced at Hannah.

"Rocky Edge?" Nancy asked. "Isn't that the estate along the river?"

"Yes, it is," Hannah Gruen replied. "Ellen says she has been offered a summer position there with the owner. If she takes it, the salary will help tremendously towards her tuition at Blackstone College of Music."

Ellen added, "My parents have suffered some serious financial reverses. They can't afford to send me and recently my father was injured in a car accident."

"I'm terribly sorry," Nancy said sympathetically. After a pause she asked, "Are you taking piano lessons?"

"No. I'm studying voice, but I do play the piano."

"Ellen has a lovely voice," Mrs Gruen put in. "A few weeks ago she sang on T.V., and her teacher is urging her to devote all her time to music and become a soloist."

"If only I could!" Ellen murmured wistfully. "But already I've borrowed a lot of money and I'm worried about how to pay it back. I want to take the position at Rocky Edge because it pays well, but the place and the people have an air of mystery about them that scares me. Besides, I'm afraid I won't be able to get along with Trixie."

"Who is she?" Nancy inquired.

"Trixie is Mrs Chatham's seven-year-old daughter," Ellen explained. "I've never met her but I understand she's unruly."

"Your job would be to look after her?"

Ellen nodded. "Mrs Chatham wants me to live there and give Trixie piano lessons. The mother is a strange person, a widow, and frustrating at times." Ellen turned to Hannah Gruen and said, "Won't you please go with me to see Mrs Chatham and talk about the position?"

The housekeeper smiled. "Why not take Nancy? She's had a lot of experience meeting strange people. If Nancy thinks it's all right for you to accept the position, I'm sure it will be."

"I'll be glad to go," Nancy said.

She was eager to help Ellen, and curious about the wealthy and eccentric Mrs Chatham.

"I don't like to put you to so much trouble," Ellen protested. "But I would appreciate having you with me."

"You're not afraid of Mrs Chatham?"

"Not exactly, and I'd try to get along with her and Trixie. I love children and enjoy working with them. At Rocky Edge I'll have time to practise my vocal work. I was told there's a small studio on the estate."

As Helen talked. Nancy could not help but wonder, "Is Ellen's decision difficult to make because of the mysterious story I heard Hannah mention? Is it connected with the position at Rocky Edge? Or is some other mystery haunting Ellen?"

As the two girls left the Drew house and walked towards the driveway, Nancy remarked to Ellen, "I heard Hannah say something about a mysterious story."

"It has to do with a map and a buried treasure," the other girl replied as they stepped into Nancy's car.

Nancy hoped to hear more about the buried treasure as they rode along, but Ellen turned the conversation towards the two girls' interest in art: one of them in music, the other in drawing and sketching.

"What are you specializing in?" she asked Nancy.

"Drawing figures and faces," Nancy replied. "As a

child I always filled in the capital o's in magazines
and newspapers with eyes, nose, mouth and ears, so I
guess Dad thought it might be a good idea if I turned
my doodling to good account!" She laughed.

Ellen said, "I hope to do the same with my music.
When Hannah Gruen worked for my family years ago,
she taught me lots of children's songs. Hannah was
really wonderful to my family. I was always sorry she
left, but when Mother and Dad returned from their
trip around the world, Mother took charge of our home
herself."

"My mother," said Nancy, "died when I was only
three and Hannah Gruen has taken care of me ever
since. She's like a member of the family."

Ellen nodded. "I know what you mean."

The car sped on past the outskirts of River Heights.
Half-way to Wayland, Nancy turned into a shady road
and presently drew up near a sign which read *Rocky
Edge*. She drove slowly up a curving tree-lined lane
towards the house.

It was a large rambling structure, half hidden from
the road by masses of high, overgrown shrubs. The
driveway led to a pillared porch.

"It's creepy here, isn't it?" Ellen remarked nervously.

"Oh, not really," Nancy replied. "No trimming has
been done on the grounds, but that gives the place
atmosphere."

"I could do without it," Ellen said uneasily as they
got out of the car.

She went ahead of Nancy and pressed the bell.
Almost at once the door was flung open. The two
callers found themselves facing a little girl.

"I don't know what you're selling!" the child cried

out. "Whatever it is we don't want any! So go away!"

"Just a minute, please," Nancy said. "We came to talk with Mrs Chatham about Miss Smith giving her daughter music lessons."

The little girl's dark eyes opened wide as she stared first at Nancy, then at Ellen. She wore her hair in two long braids, and her short dress made her thin legs look like match-sticks.

"I don't want anyone to teach me!" the child exclaimed. "There are too many now. If another one comes, I'll—I'll run away!"

"Trixie!"

Mrs Chatham, a stout woman dressed in a bright blue silk dress, had come to the door. Seizing the little girl by an arm, she pulled her away.

As Trixie began to cry, her mother said contritely, "I didn't mean to hurt you, dear, but sometimes you are impossible."

Ellen introduced Nancy to Mrs Chatham. The woman invited the callers into a living-room furnished with bizarre modern tables, chairs, and paintings. She began a lengthy account of her daughter's short-comings, regardless of the fact that the child was listening to every word.

At the first opportunity Nancy rose from her chair and asked Trixie to show her the grounds. As they walked down a shady trail, Nancy smiled at the child, recited a funny limerick, and soon had the little girl laughing gaily.

"I wish you were going to be here instead of Miss Smith," Trixie remarked. "I like you."

"You'll like Ellen too," Nancy assured her. "And I'll come to see you sometimes."

"All right. But I hope she won't try to boss me like the others did. No one can tell me what to do!"

"I'm afraid you've heard your mother say that to you so often you believe it." Nancy laughed. "Now let's forget about being naughty. Suppose you show me the rest of the grounds. Shall we go first to that little house?"

Through the trees at a spot that overlooked the river, Nancy could see the red roof of what appeared to be a tiny cottage. To her surprise Trixie held back.

"No! No! I won't go there!" she cried out.

"Why not?"

"Because the place is haunted, that's why!" The child's freckled face was tense. "I wouldn't go inside the Ship Cottage for anything!"

"The Ship Cottage?" Nancy repeated. "Is that its name?"

"It's what I call it. Please, let's go the other way."

Trixie tugged at Nancy's hand but could not make her turn in the opposite direction.

"I'm sure there's no reason why you should be afraid," Nancy said gently. "If you won't come, then I'll go alone. I'll prove to you that the place is not haunted."

"Please don't go there," the child pleaded frantically. "You'll be sorry if you do."

"What makes you so afraid of it?"

The little girl would not answer. Jerking free, she ran off in the opposite direction.

"Poor child," Nancy thought, shrugging. "I do feel sorry for her."

Nancy was sure that Trixie was watching her from a distance as she walked slowly down the path to the quaint little house. The door was unlocked and Nancy went inside. The one-room cottage was pleasant though dusty, and was lined with shelves of books. In the centre of the floor stood a very old grand piano. The ivory keys had turned yellow and cobwebs festooned the mahogany case.

"It's probably out of tune," she mused.

Nancy crossed the room and ran her fingers over the bass keys. Not a sound came from the instrument. Nancy was bewildered, and played a series of chords. Although she depressed the keys again and again no notes came out.

"That's strange!" she thought.

Nancy bent to examine the pedals to see if the piano had a spring lock that prevented the strings from being struck. There was none.

As she was about to lift up the lid of the piano Nancy noticed several model ships on the mantelpiece and others on tables.

"So that's why Trixie calls this place Ship Cottage," Nancy murmured, taking down one of the fine models from the mantel. "Undoubtedly this is the music studio Ellen mentioned."

After carefully replacing the small ship, Nancy heard a sound behind her. At the same moment she caught a reflection in the mirror above the fireplace. What she saw sent icy chills down her spine. A wall panel behind her had slid open. A bearded man with cruel, beady eyes was watching her every move.

"Leave here at once and never come back!" he warned in a rasping voice.

·2·

Curious Revelation

NANCY wheeled round and caught a fleeting glimpse of a long row of brass buttons down the front of the man's coat. The next instant the panel closed noiselessly.

As Nancy dashed towards the spot, one hand brushed the piano keys. A crash of chords broke the eerie stillness of the cottage.

Nancy tried to be calm but her heart was thumping madly. "I mustn't let myself be frightened," she told herself.

Deciding it might be dangerous to investigate the cottage further at this time, she hastily left it. Once outside, she gazed about the grounds. No one was in sight.

"I'm glad Trixie didn't come with me," she said to herself. "I've never believed in ghosts and I refuse to do so now. All the same, there's something very queer about this place."

Nancy had inherited an inquiring mind from her father, an eminent lawyer, but she also knew the wisdom of using caution in all investigations. Since solving her first mystery, Nancy had built an enviable reputation as an amateur sleuth.

Now, as she stood staring at Ship Cottage, Nancy

wondered why the piano had made no sound when her fingers had moved over the keys the first time.

"It wasn't imagination," she reflected. Just then Nancy heard her name called. Turning, she saw Ellen motioning to her from far up the path.

"Coming!" Nancy answered.

"I'm ready to leave whenever you are," Ellen announced, joining her new friend. "What became of Trixie?"

"She ran off. You know, Ellen, I rather like her," Nancy declared with sincerity.

"Mrs Chatham speaks so harshly to her," Ellen remarked. "Then the next minute she's as sweet as honey. I can't understand her."

"You've decided not to take the position for the summer?"

"I told Mrs Chatham I'd think it over."

Nancy said slowly. "There's something about Rocky Edge I don't quite like, Ellen. I wish you wouldn't come here—at least not until we've made a complete investigation of the place."

"Why, Nancy," Ellen exclaimed in astonishment, "have you learned something about Mrs Chatham?"

"Not a thing," Nancy answered. "It's mostly a feeling I have. I'll explain it later. When must you give her your answer?"

"Mrs Chatham didn't say, but I imagine she wants to know soon."

During the ride back to River Heights, Ellen sensed that Nancy was keeping something from her, and asked if this was true. Smiling, Nancy refused to divulge what she had learned.

"I'll tell my secret when you tell yours," she joked.

"But seriously, please don't accept Mrs Chatham's offer until after I talk with my dad."

"All right, I won't," Ellen promised.

Nancy drove the girl to a bus which would take her back to Blackstone College, then went to her father's office. Nancy frequently asked his assistance in solving mysteries.

Although Mr Drew was unusually busy, the tall, handsome man laid aside his papers, kissed his daughter affectionately, and listened attentively to her story about the mysterious Ship Cottage.

"You're certain you saw the open panel close again?" he asked when she had finished.

"Yes, Dad. Also, the piano was mute at first. Then later it played. How do you account for that?"

"I can't," the lawyer replied soberly. "However, I think it would be unwise for you to go there again."

"Oh, Dad!" Nancy protested in dismay. "How can I help Ellen if I don't?"

"Well, don't go alone," he amended, flashing her an understanding smile. "You're all I have, Nancy. You're very dear to me. Don't forget that."

She hugged him and promised, then asked, "Do you think it would be unwise for Ellen to accept Mrs Chatham's offer?"

"I'd say it would be foolhardy until we've checked the place thoroughly."

"I had hoped you might be able to tell me something about Rocky Edge, Dad."

Mr Drew gazed out the window for several seconds. Then he said slowly, "It seems to me I do recall some trouble a few years ago at Rocky Edge. But that would have been before the Chathams bought it."

"Who owned it previously?" Nancy asked.

"I can't remember the name of the man," her father answered, "but I think he was an inventor and there was an unusual lawsuit against him, due to one of his gadgets. As soon as I can, I'll look into the matter for you."

"I wonder if there might be some connection between the gadgets and the strange things that happened today," Nancy remarked.

"I don't know. It seems to me Mr Chatham was a friend of the owner and bought the place after the man died. Mr Chatham himself passed away less than two years ago."

Nancy was silent a moment, then asked her father what she should tell Ellen.

"Advise her to stall," Carson Drew answered promptly.

Nancy decided that instead of telephoning Ellen, she would drive to Blackstone College the next afternoon. Ellen was to be in a recital and Nancy was eager to hear her sing.

She invited her friends Bess Marvin and George Fayne to go with her and they accepted. The two girls, who were cousins, often shared Nancy's adventures. Bess, blonde and slightly plump, was a bit more timid than slim, tomboyish George.

"Oh, oh," Bess remarked as the three entered the college auditorium. "Nearly all the seats are taken."

"We'll squeeze in somewhere," Nancy declared cheerfully. "I see two places down at the front where the performers are seated."

She suggested that Bess and George go forward and take them. "I'll sit somewhere else. Introduce yourselves to Ellen Smith after the recital and tell her I'm here. We'll meet in the lobby."

As Nancy looked for a seat, she saw Mrs Chatham, half hidden beneath an enormous hat, near the rear of the auditorium. There was an empty chair beside the woman. Nancy made her way to it.

"Are you saving this seat, Mrs Chatham?" she asked, smiling.

The woman shook her head. The next moment, recognizing the newcomer, she beamed at Nancy as if they were old friends. Thus encouraged, Nancy began a conversation which she adroitly steered to a discussion of Rocky Edge. The widow mentioned its previous owner, Silas Norse.

"He must have been an interesting person. We've found several ingenious gadgets of his in the house," she said lightly.

Nancy casually mentioned her visit to Ship Cottage but did not refer to the secret panel or the man she had seen. She merely inquired if Mr Chatham had collected the ship models.

"Oh dear no! They belonged to my first husband," Mrs Chatham said with a pensive sigh. "He was such a good, kind man. It made me so sad to see those darling little boats in the house that I asked Mr Chatham to move them to the studio."

"Do you go out there frequently?" Nancy queried. "To the studio, I mean."

"Almost never."

"I suppose it was built by your late husband?"

"No," the widow replied. "It was on the property when we took over the place. I think it has been there for some time."

Nancy would have asked additional questions but just then the orchestra began to play. For an hour and a half she enjoyed the recital and was proud of Ellen Smith, whose vocal solos were the best numbers on the programme and received the most applause.

"Do come and see me some time," Mrs Chatham invited Nancy as she rose to leave.

"I'd love to," Nancy answered. "I'll try to drive to Rocky Edge within the next few days."

Just then Bess, George, and Ellen came up the aisle of the auditorium.

"Oh, Nancy!" Ellen exclaimed. "We've been looking everywhere for you."

She paused, slightly embarrassed to find herself face to face with Mrs Chatham.

"My dear, your singing was marvellous," the widow gushed. "I had no idea you were so talented. I'll be happy to have you teach music to my Trixie. You *are* accepting the position?"

Ellen glanced at Nancy, seeking a cue to the proper response.

"I—I don't know what to say," she stammered nervously. "I want to think it over."

"I must know at once!" Mrs Chatham insisted.

Fantastic Story

NANCY was afraid that since Ellen needed the money so badly she would accept the position immediately. She was greatly relieved, therefore, when the girl replied:

"I'm sorry, Mrs Chatham, but I can't possibly give you my answer for at least a week!"

"Why, that's ridiculous!" the widow protested haughtily. "You can't expect me to keep the position open indefinitely."

The situation had become an exceedingly awkward one. Nancy spoke up.

"Mrs Chatham, don't you think it would be difficult to find someone else who knows as much about music and who would be kind to Trixie?" she asked, hoping to gain time for Ellen.

Mrs Chatham admitted that this might be true. She turned again to Ellen. "All right, I'll wait a week, but no longer."

"Thank you. I promise I'll give you my answer by that time," Ellen replied.

Without waiting to be introduced to Nancy's other friends, the widow left the auditorium.

"She's a pain," George remarked with a grimace.

"I certainly wouldn't want to work for her," Bess stated.

As the girls were about to say goodbye to Ellen, she said, "Nancy, if you haven't any special plans, would you like to drive to my home and hear about the mysterious story Hannah Gruen spoke of? And I'd love to have Bess and George come too."

Nothing could have pleased Nancy more, and the other girls accepted eagerly.

"You mean you'll tell us on the way there?" Nancy asked.

"Not exactly. The secret really isn't mine to tell. It's my dad's."

Soon the group was on its way to the Smith home in Wayland. The three girls were very curious about the secret, but Ellen did not refer to the matter again.

"Do you commute to Blackstone College every day?" Bess asked Ellen presently.

"Oh no," she replied. "I board at Blackstone."

When they reached Wayland, Ellen directed Nancy to the Smith's small, old-fashioned house. As the car slowed to a stop, the girls saw a heavy-set man in his thirties, wearing a brown suit, hurriedly leaving the dwelling. His jaw was set and his eyes blazed. Without looking to left or right he jumped into a blue car at the kerb, slammed the door, and shot away.

Ellen frowned. "I—I hope nothing has happened," she stammered, quickly getting out of the convertible.

Nancy, Bess, and George watched the rapidly disappearing car. Then they followed Ellen into the house and met Mrs Smith. She was a pretty, white-haired woman in her late fifties.

"Mother, who was that man?" Ellen asked.

"His name is Rorke," Mrs Smith replied, a note of suppressed excitement in her voice. "He came to see your father about a very important matter."

"Not the map?"

"Yes, but ask your father about him."

The girls crossed the hall to a room which had been made into a combination studio and bedroom. Mr Smith lay in bed, still recuperating from his car accident. His eyes lighted with pleasure as Ellen introduced her friends.

"So glad to meet you all," he said. "Please sit down."

"What a charming room!" Bess exclaimed, her gaze wandering from the shelves of travel books to a large map of the world on one wall. "Are you interested in geography, Mr Smith?"

"He's interested in finding a treasure island!' Ellen answered eagerly. "Hannah Gruen thinks Nancy may be able to help us, Dad. She has solved lots of mysteries."

"Are you an expert at finding lost maps, young lady?" Mr Smith asked, a twinkle in his eyes.

"I've had some success with them," Nancy answered, matching his teasing tone. "But I must say, all these hints of Ellen's about a treasure are intriguing."

"Do tell your story, Dad," Ellen pleaded.

The rugged-faced man brushed a strand of hair from his forehead, then began.

"First of all, I must tell you my true name. I'm known as Tomlin Smith, although Tomlin is really my last name. Years ago I added Smith, the name of the people who adopted me after my father's death.

"My mother died when I was fourteen. Father was captain of an ocean-going freighter, the *Sea Hawk*. He had followed the sea his entire life, and his father had too. After Mother's death he was determined to take care of my twin brother and me by himself, so he took the two of us aboard the freighter. We slept in his cabin and had the run of the ship."

"You must have visited many interesting places," George remarked.

"Only half a dozen ports," Mr Smith said. "Except for a turn of luck, I'd have gone down to Davy Jones's locker along with my father."

"The ship sank?" Nancy asked, leaning forward in her chair.

"Yes, she went down in a hurricane. One of the worst on record. The seams of the old freighter cracked wide open. Every pump was manned by the crew but the ship was doomed. No one knew that better than my father."

"What did you do then?" Bess queried. "Take to the lifeboats?"

"I'm coming to that part in a minute. When my father realized that the old ship wouldn't hold together much longer, he called my twin brother John Abner and me into his cabin. Knowing he might never see his sons again, he told us our grandfather once had hidden a treasure on a small uncharted island in the Atlantic. He had left a map showing its location. My father tried to find it but never could.

"He took a parchment map from the safe," Mr Smith went on, "but instead of giving it to either of us, he tore it diagonally from corner to corner into two pieces. 'You're to share the treasure equally,' he said, 'and to make sure of that I am dividing the map in such a way that no one can find the buried chest without both sections.' "

"Then what happened?" George asked as Mr Smith paused.

"John Abner and I were put into separate lifeboats, and I never saw him again. A sudden explosion ripped the ship from bow to stern before Father was ready to leave. He went down with it.

"Along with six sailors, I landed on a small island. We lived there some months before we were picked up and brought to the United States. I tried without success to learn what had become of my brother, or where any relatives were, and finally I was adopted by a family named Smith."

"What became of your section of the map?" Nancy inquired. "Was it lost?"

"No," replied Mr Smith. "All these years I've kept it, always hoping to find my brother and hunt for the buried treasure. For a long time I had plenty of money and thought little about ever needing any. But now——"

The man looked wistfully from a window, while there was an awkward pause.

"Even if we should find the other half of the map," Mrs Smith said with a sigh, "we wouldn't have any money to look for the treasure."

"It would give me more satisfaction," her husband remarked, "to learn what became of my twin brother. As for the treasure, he or his heirs would be entitled to half of it."

"We won't worry about them just yet," said Ellen, trying to cheer her parents. "You see, Nancy, my father looked up every Tomlin he could find. Maybe his brother changed his name, and since he didn't look like Dad, nobody would think of the two being related. The map would be the only clue."

"May I see your half?" Nancy asked.

Mr Smith requested his daughter to bring the paper

from the top drawer of a desk in his study upstairs. Presently she returned with a piece of yellow parchment. Eagerly Nancy bent to examine the curious markings.

"Right here is our treasure island, as I call it," Tomlin Smith indicated, "but as you see, the name has been torn off. All tha appears on my half is 'lm Island,' which isn't much help."

Nancy studied the parchment for a few moments, then asked Mr Smith, "Would you mind if I made a copy of it?"

"Not at all," he answered. "Only I'm sure you can't make much out of it. As I told Mr Rorke today, it's not worth a nickel without my brother's half."

"Was he the man who drove away in the blue car?" Nancy asked.

"Yes, he left the house just as you girls arrived."

"Mother said he came to see you about the map," Ellen declared. "How did he learn about it?"

"Mr Rorke claimed he'd heard the story from the son of a man who was first mate on my father's sunken freighter—an officer by the name of Tom Gambrell. Rorke offered to buy my section of the map. Said he wanted it as a souvenir."

"You didn't agree to sell your half?" Nancy asked, afraid the answer might be yes.

"No, I told Rorke I wouldn't sell at any price," Mr Smith said. "Even if the parchment is worthless, it was my father's last gift. I'll always keep it."

"I'm glad," Nancy said in relief. "Of course I know nothing about Mr Rorke, but I didn't like his looks. Also, since you changed your name, how did he find you?"

"That's a good question," said Ellen's father. "I never thought to ask him. But he'll probably be back and I'll put it up to him."

"Did you show him your piece of the map?" Nancy inquired.

"Yes, I had Mrs Smith bring it downstairs," Ellen's father replied. "But Rorke saw it only for a second; not long enough to remember what was on it, if that's what you're afraid of."

Nancy said no more and busied herself copying the torn map while the others talked about the recital. Bess and George spoke glowingly of Ellen's singing and her parents smiled proudly. Presently Mrs Smith appeared with a tray of refreshments.

Soon afterwards the callers rose to leave. Nancy carefully folded the copy of the treasure map and put it into her bag.

She smiled at Mr Smith. "I don't promise to figure this out, but it will be good mental exercise and I'm eager to start working on some way to find your brother."

The callers said goodbye and left. Nancy drove towards River Heights. Presently they stopped for a red traffic light. Directly ahead, waiting at the same intersection, was a blue saloon.

"That looks like the car we saw at the Smith place!" George exclaimed.

"It *is* the same one! The driver is that Mr Rorke!" Nancy cried.

The traffic light turned green, and the blue saloon was away in a flash. Nancy's car was equally fast and kept directly behind Mr Rorke.

"You're going to follow him?" Bess asked nervously.

"I'd like to find out more about him," Nancy replied. "It's my hunch he has a special interest in the Smiths' treasure map that he's not telling."

Bess and George were inclined to agree. As the man's car raced ahead and turned corners recklessly it was very evident that he was trying to lose Nancy. Twice Rorke glanced uneasily over his shoulder.

"He knows we're trailing him," George commented. "But why should it worry him?"

"Nancy, do be careful," Bess cautioned, gripping the edge of the seat. "We're coming to a railway crossing."

Signals warned of an approaching train. Knowing that it would be dangerous to attempt a crossing, Nancy stopped. The blue saloon, however, shot ahead on to the track.

·4·

A Strange Lawsuit

BESS closed her eyes, expecting a crash. But the driver ahead crossed the tracks with only seconds to spare.

"He drives that bus of his as if the police were after him," George commented.

As the long freight train thundered past, Nancy looked between the cars to see if Mr Rorke were in sight. But there was no sign of the blue car.

"We've lost him now," she declared gloomily. "I may as well turn back."

Nancy drove to River Heights and dropped George and Bess at their homes. In a few minutes she reached her own house, which was set back from the street and was reached by a curving driveway. Mr Drew's car rolled in right behind her.

"Hello, Nancy," the lawyer greeted his daughter fondly. "I came home early today—had a rather hard session in court."

Nancy and her father strolled through the garden.

"Dad, let's sit down here," she suggested after a few moments, indicating a stone bench. "I have something to show you."

"A letter from Ned Nickerson?" he teased. "Or is it from a new admirer?"

Nancy laughed. "Neither. It's something I copied today from part of a map of a treasure island!"

"Treasure island?" Mr Drew repeated in disbelief. "You're joking."

"No, it's genuine, Dad."

Nancy handed the paper to him, then related everything she had learned at the Tomlin Smith home. Anxiously she awaited her father's comment.

"I don't like the sound of this Rorke fellow," the lawyer said. "He could be dangerous. I'd much rather help the Smith family in a financial way than have you concerned with a lost treasure that Rorke's also after."

"There's more than a map and treasure involved," Nancy told him. "Mr Smith wants me to find his long-lost twin brother, John Abner Tomlin. He's heir to half the treasure their grandfather buried, and Mr Smith insists they must share equally, as his father wished."

"That difficulty could be solved easily by putting half the money in a trust fund," Mr Drew remarked. "But locating the treasure is a remote possibility."

"The half map Mr Smith possesses appears to be authentic, Dad. My copy probably isn't good enough to convince you."

"I can't tell much from this," he admitted. "The parchment was torn in such a way that one can't figure out what any of the names or directions mean. Have you tried comparing it with an atlas?"

"Not yet, Dad. Let's do it now."

Carson Drew accompanied Nancy to his study and for some time they pored over several maps. When Hannah Gruen announced dinner, the lawyer was so engrossed that he was reluctant to give up the search.

"Old Captain Tomlin was a clever fellow," he conceded. "By tearing the map as he did, the shape of the island is destroyed, so now it's practically impossible to determine its location without the missing section."

"I'm glad you said 'practically.' " Nancy chuckled and led the way to the dining-room. "You see, Dad, I mean to attempt the impossible. On Monday I'll do some sleuthing at the public library."

On Sunday morning the Drews went to church, then spent the afternoon relaxing at home. Nancy kept thinking about the mystery and remarked to her father, "If the treasure is so hard to find it could mean no one has dug it up yet!"

"Right!" Mr Drew chuckled.

The following morning Nancy spent two hours at the library examining old atlases and historic records. Although the librarian permitted her access to some old and precious maps, she could find no chart which bore any resemblance to the scrap in her possession.

Disappointed, Nancy turned to business directories and biographies. She carefully studied the names listed.

"There's not a John Abner Tomlin among them," Nancy sighed.

Next, she consulted an old book on ships lost at sea. It contained a brief account of the sinking of the *Sea Hawk*. Captain Abner Tomlin, age forty-five was in charge of the freighter. There also was a list of the officers and sailors who had shipped aboard. As Nancy carefully copied the names, she noticed there was no Tom Gambrell listed.

"That's point number one against Mr. Rorke," she decided, rising to leave.

Next, Nancy went to the newspaper office of the *River Heights Gazette* and asked if she might look through their files of old issues. Soon she was busy searching for stories concerning the Chatham estate. Without much trouble she found an article reporting the sale of Rocky Edge, after the owner Silas Norse had died.

"Now to find out if there are any items about strange gadgets there," the young detective told herself, turning sheet after sheet.

Finally her eyes lighted upon a startling headline:

BURGLAR STARTS LAWSUIT
Thief Injured at Estate Claims Damages

The story went on to tell how one Spike Doty had broken into the home of Silas Norse. As he was about to escape with valuable loot, he had been caught between sliding panels and injured rather badly. Though held for robbery, Doty had made a claim for damages.

"I wonder if he ever collected!" Nancy thought. "I'll bet he didn't because he was a trespasser!"

She hunted further and found a photograph and an article about the inventor himself. There were pictures of various rooms in his home, showing sliding panels, secret closets, and several gadgets. Nancy was on the point of deciding that Rocky Edge was no place for Ellen Smith when she read that Mr Norse was planning to have all these things removed.

"But he forgot about the secret panel in Ship Cottage," she thought, recalling her adventure there. "I can vouch for that! And maybe Mr Norse didn't remove some of the others!"

Nancy decided to talk with Ellen about her sleuthing so far. Upon reaching home she telephoned at once and was invited to come over to dinner and spend the night in the Blackstone dormitory.

When she finished the conversation, Nancy told Hannah the plans. "And tomorrow I'm going to the Emerson College dance with Ned, you know. It's the big year-end party of the Dramatic Club. I'm so sorry Bess and George couldn't accept Burt's and Dave's invitations. The boys have decided to attend a fraternity convention instead, so I won't see them."

"I'm sorry too," said Hannah. "The girls would have been company for you on the long ride. By the way, Nancy, that new dress you're going to travel in hasn't been shortened yet. Suppose you put it on right now and I'll get the correct length."

While Hannah marked the new hemline with chalk, Nancy told her what she had learned at the library.

"I don't like the sound of any of it," Hannah remarked when Nancy had finished. "Ellen had better not go to the Chathams, and the Smiths ought to beware of that Mr Rorke."

While waiting for the dress to be hemmed, Nancy did various chores around the house. Then she packed her suitcase and finally phoned her father to say goodbye.

"Have a good time with Ellen and at Emerson, and be careful, dear," he cautioned her.

"Will do," she promised.

Nancy spent two hours at art school classes, then started for Blackstone, reaching Ellen's dormitory just before suppertime.

"Oh, I'm so glad to see you!" Ellen said warmly. "Come and meet my friends. By the way, would you mind going to my home tonight to sleep? We're giving an operetta here tomorrow and I've promised to bring over several things to use as stage props. And a couple of costumes."

"I don't mind a bit," Nancy replied. "We'll have a better chance to talk if we're alone."

Nancy thoroughly enjoyed herself at dinner and later at the dress rehearsal. It was after ten before she and Ellen got away and eleven when they reached Wayland.

"I imagine Mother and Dad have gone to bed," Ellen remarked as Nancy turned the car into the Smiths' street. "They seldom stay up late."

As she had surmised, her house was in total darkness.

"Do you have your key, Ellen?"

"Oh, I forgot it!" she exclaimed. "I'll have to ring the bell."

No one answered. After a long wait Ellen tried again, but still there was no response.

"They must be sleeping soundly," she commented.

"Let's try the back door," Nancy suggested. "If that's locked we may be able to get in through a window."

Moving quietly so that the neighbours would not be disturbed, the girls went round the house. Nancy halted suddenly, clutching Ellen's hand.

"Look!" she whispered tensely.

A tall ladder leaned against the house wall, leading to an open window on the second floor. As the girls stared at it, a man's shadowy figure moved stealthily down the rungs!

- 5 -

The Stolen Parchment

"A BURGLAR!" Nancy whispered into Ellen's ear. "Don't make a sound! Maybe we can catch him."

Remaining motionless, the girls waited until the man had nearly reached the base of the ladder. Then, at a signal from Nancy, they made a concerted rush for him.

After the first moment of surprise he began to struggle. With one push he sent Ellen reeling backwards into a clump of dwarf evergreens. Nancy held on, but the muscular man was too strong for her.

"Let go!" he ordered harshly. "If you don't, I'll get rough!"

Headlights from a passing car momentarily focused on the struggling pair, and in that second Nancy caught a glimpse of the man's bearded face and angry eyes.

"I won't let you go!" she defied him.

In the wild struggle the ladder was pushed away from the wall. It toppled, narrowly missing Ellen, and struck the garage with a loud crash.

"Help! Help!" screamed Nancy, hoping that her cry would awaken the neighbours.

Instantly the prowler clapped his hand across her mouth. Shaking free from her grasp, he lifted her bodily and threw her down on the grass.

Nancy fell so hard that the breath was knocked from

her, but she struggled to her feet. By this time the man had run across the lawn and disappeared beyond a hedge.

"Are you all right, Nancy?" Ellen gasped, limping towards her friend.

"Yes, but it's too bad that intruder got away."

"Oh, I hope he didn't steal anything," Ellen said.

In the house next door lights were being snapped on. The upper floor of the Smith home suddenly was illuminated. Ellen's mother raised a window and called to ask what was wrong.

"Hello, Mother," said Ellen. "I'm afraid our home has been robbed. Nancy and I just tried to capture a man who was coming out of the house!"

"Oh, goodness me!" Mrs Smith exclaimed.

"We couldn't hold him. Is Dad all right?"

There was no answer. The girls guessed that Mrs Smith had run downstairs to her husband's room. A few minutes later she unlocked the back door. By this time several neighbours had arrived to find out the cause of the commotion. Nancy explained what had happened, and one man summoned the police. Ellen and Nancy found Mr Smith in a state of nervous alarm.

"Probably my desk has been rifled!" he cried out. "I'm sure the parchment map is gone!"

"Now don't get excited, Tomlin," Mrs Smith said soothingly. "Maybe the girls got here in time to prevent a robbery."

"If I were you I'd check to make sure," Nancy urged. "The man may have ransacked several rooms in your house."

While she and Ellen counted the silverware, Mrs Smith hastened upstairs. In a few minutes she returned and one glance at her stricken face told the girls that the precious map was gone.

"I was afraid the map was what the prowler came for," Nancy commented. "Maybe that man Rorke sent him."

"That's what I call a low-down trick," Mr Smith fumed. "Now who could that scamp be, and why should he want the map?"

"Obviously to obtain the treasure!" exclaimed Ellen. "Oh, Dad, the parchment *must* have genuine value! And to think we've lost it!"

"You forgot that I made a copy of the original," Nancy reminded the others. "It's crudely drawn but fairly accurate and I have it with me."

Mr Smith said gratefully, "You're a lifesaver."

To Nancy's embarrassment he introduced her to the neighbours who had gathered on the front porch and told them how brave she and Ellen had been.

As soon as the police arrived, a Sergeant Holmes introduced himself and Officer Mentor. He asked the girls to describe the intruder. Ellen could remember nothing about him but his surprising strength. Nancy however, not only provided the police with an excellent description of the heavy-set thirty-year-old prowler, but drew a rough sketch of his face.

Nancy had recognized the close resemblance between the intruder and the "apparition" of Ship Cottage but did not mention this.

"Say, you're something of an artist!" the sergeant said admiringly. "A good observer, too! This fellow looks like one of our old friends."

"Spike Doty!" the other policeman added, studying the sketch.

"The same Spike Doty who broke into Rocky Edge a few years ago?" Nancy asked.

"He's the one. Has a record a mile long, and is wanted for another robbery."

Sergeant Holmes said, "He's a sailor, and a fairly good one when he's willing to work."

The officers went outside to make an investigation. Just before they left, Nancy walked out on to the front porch. She saw a man and a woman dart from the side of the house and hurry to a car which had been parked up the street. The car was too far away for her to distinguish either the make or the licence.

"That's queer," she thought. "I wonder if they were just curious bystanders or if they had some part in the robbery."

In the morning she and Ellen had breakfast about nine o'clock, helped with the dishes, and then drove to Blackstone College. They assisted in setting the stage for the operetta and had lunch. At four o'clock Nancy said she must start for Emerson College to attend the dance with Ned Nickerson.

"I'm staying there only one night," she said to Ellen in parting. "On my way home I'll stop at Rocky Edge and investigate some more."

"Thanks so much. I do need a salary comparable to the one Mrs Chatham offers so I can come back here next fall," Ellen said wistfully.

Nancy drove leisurely along a winding country road. A grey car followed some distance behind. She did not give it a second thought until she had gone several miles.

"Why doesn't that car pass me?" Nancy wondered.

Deliberately she slowed up, but the car behind also slackened pace. With increasing uneasiness Nancy remembered that she had the precious copy of Tomlin Smith's map in her bag.

"It's time that I find out what's what!" she thought. "We'll play a little game of hide-and-seek."

Again Nancy slackened her pace, turning into a paved side road. She felt certain that unless the occupants of the grey car were trailing her they would not make the turn. Watching in the mirror, she was alarmed to see the car leave the main road.

"I am being followed," she thought anxiously. "And they're gaining on me, too!"

By this time the grey car was so near that she could see two persons in the front seat, a man and a woman. Nancy recognized them as the couple who had hurried out of the Smith driveway the night before! She tried in vain to read the licence plate which was covered with mud. Gradually, so as not to reveal her concern, Nancy speeded up but was unable to lose her pursuers.

"They mean business," she thought grimly. "If I don't lose them quickly, they'll probably try to stop me when we come to the first lonely stretch."

Directly ahead was a dirt road which Nancy knew led to the town of Hamilton, two miles away. Without hesitation she turned into it, even though she realized it would take her away from Emerson.

Another burst of speed put her far ahead of the pursuing car. Nevertheless, as she entered the town of Hamilton she saw that the man and woman had not given up the chase.

Nancy looked in vain for police headquarters. Finally she parked in front of the bus station and ran inside. Entering a telephone booth, she called Ned Nickerson at Emerson College and told him of her predicament.

"I am being followed!" Nancy thought anxiously

"You stay there until I come," Ned advised. "A bus leaves for Hamilton in fifteen minutes. If I hurry I can catch it. Whatever you do, don't give that couple a chance to approach you."

"I'll be safe enough until you get here," Nancy said to reassure him. "There are several people around and I doubt the couple would try anything out in the open."

Even as she hung up the phone, the grey car parked some distance behind her own. Uneasily Nancy sat down in the waiting-room. Recalling that she had failed to leave a copy of the map with Mr Smith, she took a notebook from her purse and began to sketch.

Nancy became so absorbed in her work that she did not glance up until a woman sat down beside her. The newcomer was about thirty-five years old, stout, and had a cold, steady gaze which rested on Nancy's notebook.

"She's the one who was in the grey car!" the young detective said to herself.

Getting up abruptly, Nancy thrust both drawings into her handbag and hurriedly left the bus station. A glance revealed that the woman's accomplice was waiting nearby, so she started walking in the opposite direction.

"I'll be safe if I stay within sight of other people," Nancy reasoned, clutching her handbag. "If it's the map they want, I must finish the second copy quickly and put it somewhere."

A block away Nancy came to a large department store. Turning into it, she made her way to the third floor. She located a telephone booth and closed herself into it.

"I'll be okay here for a few minutes," she thought,

opening her bag. "Now to finish copying the map."

She completed the sketch in less than five minutes. Realizing that both drawings could be stolen, Nancy came to a sudden decision. She sealed her original sketch in an envelope which she addressed to her father, then discovered she had no stamp.

"I'll post it at the post office. I may be followed, but I must take the risk."

Nancy hoped that she had not been observed entering the store, but when she emerged from the building, the woman and the man were waiting. As she walked hurriedly along the street they followed in their car.

"They're afraid to approach me now," she reasoned, "but if I'm alone for a minute I'll have trouble. I wonder if they're in league with Spike Doty."

Nancy entered the post office, bought a stamp, and posted the map. She remained in the building for a few minutes, allowing herself exactly enough time to reach the bus station before Ned was due to arrive.

Her watch proved to be accurate, for as she came within view of the station she saw three buses coming down the street. With a sigh of relief she quickened her step and joined the crowd of passengers waiting to get on.

The farthest bus finally came to a standstill. Nancy caught a glimpse of Ned alighting from the last bus and waved to him.

As the passengers pushed towards the first bus, someone brushed against her. Nancy felt a slight tug on her arm. Startled, she whirled round in time to see a man running down the street.

"My bag!" she cried out. "My bag has been stolen!"

·6·

Sudden Danger

At Nancy's cry of distress a number of people turned round, but no one tried to stop the fleeing thief. He was soon out of sight. A policeman appeared on the scene and questioned Nancy about the bag snatcher.

"His car's over there!" she exclaimed, pointing. "And the woman with him—" Nancy stopped speaking abruptly. "Why—it's gone!" She felt sick over the turn of events.

"Suppose you tell me the whole story," the policeman said kindly.

Nancy did not wish to disclose the details of her recent adventure and its connection with the current mystery. She stated simply, "A woman and a man followed me here in a grey saloon. I believe he was the same one who snatched my bag. He's about six feet tall, sandy-haired, and very thin.

"The woman is about thirty-five, average height, and rather heavy. She has light-brown hair and hazel eyes."

Nancy paused, then added. "I'd say the man is older than she is. They both wore navy-blue suits."

"Did you have much money with you?"

"Practically none. There were a few personal articles, though, that I hate to lose."

As Nancy was talking to the policeman, Ned Nickerson, a handsome, athletic young man, came through the group.

"Hello, Nancy," he greeted her anxiously. "What happened?"

"I'll tell you all about it in a minute," she promised.

Nancy thanked the officer for his help, then she and Ned went to a quiet corner of the waiting-room where they could talk.

"Now tell me everything," he insisted.

When Nancy finished relating her afternoon adventures, Ned asked, "Do you have any idea what they are after?"

"This." From her dress pocket she removed a copy of Tomlin Smith's map and showed it to him. "When I was in the store's telephone booth, I transferred my money and this paper from my handbag to my pocket."

Ned studied the crude drawing. "It looks like a lesson in geography. Half a lesson at that."

"That's just what it is—half a map showing where a treasure is buried."

"Belonging to Captain Kidd?"

"I know it may sound fantastic, but this is a clue to an inheritance buried on some Atlantic island," Nancy declared.

Next, she told him the entire story of Rocky Edge, its eccentric owners, and the vanishing man in the music studio.

Ned grinned. "Guess I won't be seeing much of you for a while with two mysteries to solve—especially when you're off to some lonely island." Then, with a wide grin, he added, "Unless we go sailing for gold together!"

The two laughed and Ned glanced at his watch. If

they were to reach Emerson College before dinner-time, they must leave at once.

"Do you mind delaying a few minutes longer while I buy a bag and a few things I must replace?" Nancy asked.

"Give you fifteen minutes," he conceded.

She completed her shopping, then they started off in Nancy's car. At the fraternity house, she was greeted by Mrs Haines, the housemother, and several young women. All of them had been invited to spend the night.

As Nancy started upstairs to shower and dress for the dance, someone called out, "Telephone for Nancy Drew!"

"For me?" she asked in surprise, retracing her steps. "Maybe it's Dad."

The caller proved to be Ellen Smith, who spoke in an agitated voice.

"Nancy, I'm sorry to bother you," she apologized. "It's about Mrs Chatham. She came to see me at college today and absolutely insists that I give her my decision about the position in three days. What shall I tell her?"

"I'll talk to Mrs Chatham tomorrow," Nancy promised. "Don't do anything until I see you."

"I really can't afford to turn down the job."

"I understand," Nancy assured her. "Don't worry about it, Ellen. If it seems unwise for you to take the position, I'll try to find another one for you."

"Oh, I knew you'd think of something," the other girl said gratefully. "You're a darling."

After Ellen had hung up, Nancy decided to phone her home and tell her father what had happened.

Hannah Gruen answered and said Mr Drew was not there.

"I'm so glad you called," the housekeeper said, her voice unsteady.

"What's wrong? You sound upset."

"About half an hour ago a man phoned. He didn't give his name, but he had the most unpleasant voice!"

"What did he say?"

" 'Lay off the Tomlin matter or you'll be sorry.' Those were his exact words. Oh, Nancy, that warning was meant for you. And to think that I suggested you take an interest in the Smiths' problems!"

After a somewhat lengthy conversation Nancy convinced the housekeeper that there was no immediate cause for alarm. She did not mention the incident at the Hamilton bus station, knowing it would only add to Mrs Gruen's uneasiness.

Later, as Nancy was dressing, she speculated as to who the strange caller might have been. Spike Doty or the bag snatcher? Finally she decided to forget both for the evening.

When Nancy descended the stairs in her striking white dress, she saw Ned's face light up with admiration. "Wow!" he exclaimed with a smile. "May I have the honour?"

"You may," Nancy replied.

The couple linked arms and strolled into the main dining-room which was attractively decorated in the college's colours of purple and orange. Several of Ned's classmates gave Nancy an admiring glance and an exaggerated nod of approval to her escort.

After dinner there was an inter-fraternity dance in the gymnasium. Nancy thoroughly enjoyed herself.

During an intermission Nancy noticed one of Ned's fraternity brothers walking towards them.

"I don't know him very well," Ned whispered. "He came to Emerson just this year. His name is Bill Tomlin."

"Tomlin?" Nancy asked.

"Why, yes, do you know him?"

"I didn't tell you, Ned, but the old sea captain had that same last name. They're probably not even distantly related but I must check every possible clue."

Bill Tomlin, pleasant and humorous, asked to dance with her. As they moved across the floor, she casually inquired if any member of his family had followed the sea.

"My grandfather's brother was a sea captain," he replied. "He had twin sons and I understand one of them was a sea captain. I don't know what became of the other brother."

Nancy tried not to show her mounting excitement. She asked, "Do you know if the captain is still living and where he might be found?"

Before her dance partner could reply, the music stopped abruptly. The bass drum thumped loudly and the chairman of the dance committee, Jeff Garwin, rose to speak.

"Your attention, please!" he said over the microphone. "I have an important announcement to make. The next event on our programme is the presentation of a pantomime produced by members of the Emerson College Dramatic Club.

"As you all know, it is our custom each year to select an attractive young lady to preside over the event.

She will wear the Festival Robe and Crown. After careful consideration by a committee of faculty and students, a choice has been made."

A hush fell over the audience as the announcer paused a long moment.

"Will Miss Nancy Drew please come to the stage," he said, smiling down at the girl.

The students clapped and whistled. Though startled, Nancy responded with poise and mounted the improvised stage. She donned a white robe, a golden paper crown, and accepted the seat of honour.

Lights were dimmed and the presentation of the pantomime began. It was impossible to tell who the players were, because they all wore black masks. Nancy thought she could identify Ned as a Black Demon, but before she could be sure, all the lights were suddenly extinguished.

"Hey, what's the big idea?" masculine voices called. "Is this part of the show?"

After several minutes of confusion the lights were turned on.

"I'm sorry for the interruption," the announcer said in apology. "Someone thought he'd play a practical joke, I guess."

"And steal the queen?" Bill Tomlin added, gazing towards the stage.

The draped chair which Nancy had occupied was vacant.

"Where is she?" Ned demanded, stepping forward in alarm and removing his mask.

The announcer's voice was unsteady as he spoke. "No doubt Nancy Drew has stepped outside for a breath of air."

The explanation seemed to satisfy the audience, but Bill and Ned realized that Jeff did not believe this himself. The three hurried outside and began a search for the missing girl.

But by now Nancy was several miles away, a captive in a grey car which raced over the countryside. When the lights had been extinguished during the pantomime, a masked man, whom Nancy assumed to be one of the players, had glided to her side.

"Come with me!" he had commanded.

Thinking that it was part of the show, Nancy had obeyed. No sooner had she reached the hall than a woman appeared from behind a screen of palms. The pair were the same couple who had trailed her to Hamilton and snatched her handbag! They gagged Nancy and hustled her into the rear of a waiting car. The man jumped into the driver's seat.

"Don't make a move or try to escape," he rasped as the woman removed the gag. "Just hand over the map and you won't be harmed."

Nancy squirmed sideways on the car seat, peering at the woman who gripped her arm.

"So it was you who switched off the lights," Nancy remarked.

"Just hand over that map or I'll take it from you," the woman said.

"I have no map."

"Don't try to pull anything on us. You thought you were so clever removing it from your handbag this afternoon. Where is it?"

"I'm not in the habit of carrying maps in party dresses!" Nancy countered.

"All right, don't tell us!" the woman snapped. "But

understand this. You're going to be our prisoner until we get it."

The threat filled Nancy with despair. She did not doubt the couple's intentions. If they should contact her father, he would turn over his copy of the map to insure her release.

Nancy set her jaw grimly. She must think of some way out of this situation!

·7·

Ghosts

THE car was approaching a traffic light. Nancy decided that if the signal turned red she would make a desperate attempt to escape. First she must distract the woman's attention.

"It would be very foolish of you to hold me prisoner," she said in a firm voice. "Especially since the original map has been stolen."

"We know all about that," the man answered.

"Perhaps you engineered the theft," Nancy said coldly.

"Not on your life! I overheard Tomlin Smith tell about the map and the duplicate you made of it. You've got it!"

The woman added, "You sneaked it out of your bag this afternoon!"

"Are you sure I was the one who removed it? Maybe your friend can explain what happened to it. Why don't you ask him?" Nancy suggested.

The man slammed on the brakes to keep from passing through the red traffic light. Angrily he glared over his shoulder at Nancy.

"What are you trying to do? Stir up trouble?" he demanded. "I don't know what you're talking about. I never took that map from your pocketbook."

"Your conscience seems to be bothering you," Nancy said.

"Fred, if you think you can double-cross me—" the woman shouted. "If you have—"

"Oh, shut up, Irene!" the man bellowed. "You make me tired!"

"You're working with Doty and leaving me out!" she accused him, her voice rising to a shrill pitch. "You want to get all the money for yourself and cut me out!"

With the two absorbed in their quarrel, Nancy knew this was her opportunity to escape. In a moment the traffic signal would flash green.

Nancy tore herself from the woman's vice-like grasp and jerked open the car door. She tumbled out on to the ground, tripping over her white robe, but picked herself up and began to run.

"Stop her, Fred!" Nancy heard the woman shout. "Don't let her get away!"

Nancy was frantic. On either side of the highway were deep ditches and high fences separating her from open fields. She kept running but knew that if her agile captor took after her on foot, she would be caught. A second later a car's headlights flashed behind her.

"The kidnappers won't dare bother me with witnesses in the vicinity," she thought. "And maybe I can get a ride!"

Nancy knew that normally it was unwise to signal strangers for a ride, but in this emergency she must try to stop the approaching car! She held up her arms and waved them. There was a squeal of brakes. The car drew up a few yards away.

"Don't stop, Henry!" cried the woman beside the driver. "Go on! You know you shouldn't pick up hitch-hikers. Besides, this one's dressed up like a ghost!"

Nancy had forgotten about her costume. Fearful that the couple would not help her, she called out:

"Wait! I'm not a ghost! Please wait!"

To her great relief the driver obeyed. Nancy ran to the car. Without waiting for an invitation she climbed into the rear seat.

"Oh, thank you," she said, gasping for breath. "The people in that car back there tried to kidnap me. Drive on quickly, please!"

"What!" the pair exclaimed in astonishment, and the woman added, "Why are you dressed up like that?"

Nancy explained quickly, and noted with relief that the kidnappers were making no attempt to pursue her.

"You don't say!" the driver remarked. "I suppose the kidnapping was like an initiation or something?"

Nancy was about to explain but decided she did not want to cause the couple further alarm. Instead she said, "I'm just so glad you came by. Would it be out of your way to take me to the Emerson gymnasium?"

"I'd be glad to drop you there," the man replied.

Twenty minutes later Nancy was running up the drive towards the college building.

As she did, someone called from behind a clump of bushes. "Nancy, is it you?"

She recognized Ned's voice and said, laughing, "Yes. Did you miss me?"

"Don't be funny. We were worried sick," said Bill Tomlin, who was with Ned. "What happened to you?"

"I was kidnapped. Ned, it was the same couple who followed me this afternoon. But we must keep the whole thing quiet."

"You mean you're not going to notify the police?" Ned demanded disapprovingly.

"No, not until I've talked to Dad. For now we must pass off my disappearance as a joke."

The boys frowned at each other, then Ned spoke. "Jeff Garwin went inside a minute ago to call police headquarters. I suppose you want me to try to stop him."

"Please do, Ned," Nancy replied. "I don't want any publicity."

While Ned hurried into the building, she and Bill Tomlin walked at a more leisurely pace. Nancy related the highlights of her harrowing experience. Then she told Bill of her search for the missing Captain John Abner Tomlin. "Can you give me any clues?"

"Captain Tomlin died when I was very young. I really don't know much about him or his twin brother. My father could tell you a lot more."

"I suppose your parents live some distance from here," Nancy commented thoughtfully.

"No," Bill said. "In Kirkland."

"Why, I'll be passing through there on my way to River Heights!"

"Then why not stop and talk to my father? He owns the Elite Department Store and no doubt will be in his office there."

"I hope he won't think I'm prying—"

"He'd be glad to see you," Bill declared. "I'll phone him and say you're coming."

Nancy was glad that Bill Tomlin had taken her curiosity so casually. She did not want to divulge any information about the Smiths or their possible inheritance.

When Nancy finally returned to the gymnasium, several young men and girls swarmed around her. She answered their questions, giving the impression that her disappearance was nothing more than a fun adventure connected with the pantomime. Her explanation seemed to satisfy everyone and once more the party got into full swing.

In the morning Nancy was awake early, eager to start for Kirkland. To her disappointment she did not see Bill Tomlin again, but Ned brought a message from him.

"Bill says his dad will be expecting you."

"Good," said Nancy as she stepped into her car. "I've had a wonderful time, Ned. Thanks a million for everything."

"I wish you could have stayed until after lunch," he complained good-naturedly. "Please don't take any short-cuts. Stick to the main roads and you won't be kidnapped!"

"You can depend on my obeying orders, sir." Nancy laughed. "And thanks for a grand time."

The trip to Kirkland took less than an hour and Nancy was certain that she had not been followed. Without difficulty she located the Elite Department Store and in a short time was escorted to Mr Tomlin's office.

"Good morning," Bill's father said cordially, motioning her to a chair. "I understand you're interested in the Tomlin family history."

"Yes, I am. Friends of mine are trying to trace some lost family history. May I ask you a few questions?"

"I'll do my best to answer them."

Nancy inquired about Captain Tomlin, the third in

his family to follow the sea. The store owner confirmed that the man had died many years ago while on a voyage to Japan.

"He was Captain John Tomlin and was a cousin of mine," he remarked. "A wonderful man. I thought a lot of him."

"Did he have a middle name?"

"I'm sure he had one but it has slipped my mind at the moment."

Nancy went on, "Your son told me he had a twin brother."

"Yes," Mr Tomlin replied. "I don't know whether he's dead or alive."

"Did Captain John Tomlin leave a widow and children?" was Nancy's next question.

"He married but had no children to my knowledge. I've never heard what happened to his wife. She disappeared after his death."

"What was Captain Tomlin like?" Nancy queried. "Did he have any hobbies?"

"Yes, he enjoyed collecting things—rare sea shells for instance. I still have one he gave me. I've kept it all these years."

Mr Tomlin opened a desk drawer. After hunting through a pile of papers, he brought out a small colourful shell.

"This is called a Lion's Paw," he said, offering it to Nancy. "It's a type of clam found in East Indian waters. Its Latin name is Hippopus Maculatus!"

"It's very pretty! Did the captain have other hobbies?" Nancy asked.

"He was considered an authority on old songs of the sea. He could sing dozens of them."

"Then he must have had a good voice," Nancy commented. She was interested in this piece of information; it might be a clue.

Everything she had learned seemed to confirm her idea that Captain John Tomlin was Tomlin Smith's missing brother John Abner. Feeling that she owed Bill's father an explanation for asking so many questions, she mentioned her theory to him.

"I should like to meet Tomlin Smith," he said. "I wonder if the two were identical twins."

"I don't believe so. As far as I know there is no resemblance between them."

"Somewhere at home I have a photograph of Captain Tomlin," the store owner said thoughtfully. "Would that be of any help to you?"

"Oh, yes. Mr Smith should be able to identify the picture."

"Then I'll post it to you if I can find it," Mr Tomlin promised. "Just write your address on this pad."

Nancy was elated by the successful interview, feeling that she had taken a long step towards solving the mystery about the owner of the other half of the map. As she walked lightheartedly through the store towards an exit she decided to phone Bess, and went to a booth.

"Hi, Bess!" she began. "I'm on my way to Mrs Chatham's estate, but Dad doesn't want me to go there alone. Could you and George meet me there in half an hour?"

"I'll be glad to come," Bess answered instantly. "I'll call George."

"This is what I'd like you to do for me," Nancy said. "I'm going to investigate the music studio but I don't want Mrs Chatham to know it. Could you both keep her engaged in conversation?"

"Will do," Bess promised. "Please be careful."

After chatting for a moment longer, Nancy left the store. She drove on towards Rocky Edge, arriving ahead of her friends. As she glanced up the road, wondering how long they would be delayed, she was startled to hear a shrill scream. The cry had come from the area near the building which Trixie called Ship Cottage.

Nancy sprang from her car and dashed towards the spot. Emerging from among the oak trees, she caught a glimpse of the little girl. Trixie Chatham was running away from the studio, her hair blowing wildly across her fact.

"Ghosts! Ghosts!" she screamed. "I saw 'em! They're in the cottage!"

The child did not see Nancy nor hear her soothing voice as she called to the little girl. In panic Trixie scrambled through a hedge, straight into the path of an oncoming car!

·8·

Nancy Investigates

INSTINCTIVELY Nancy darted after the terrified child. She seized her by the hand and jerked the little girl from the roadway just as the car whizzed by.

"Let me go!" Trixie cried, trying to pull away. Then, seeing who her rescuer was, she relaxed slightly. "Oh, it's you," she said.

"What's the matter, Trixie?" Nancy asked gently. "You were almost run down by that car."

The little girl began to sob, her thin body shaking. While Nancy was trying to comfort her, another car approached and drew up alongside the road. George was driving; Bess sat beside her.

"What's wrong?" Bess asked, stepping from the car. "Has Trixie been hurt?"

"No, she's all right," Nancy answered, "but she had a narrow escape. Something frightened her and she ran into the path of a car."

"What was it that scared you, Trixie?" George asked.

Trixie moved nearer Nancy, away from the other two girls.

"It—it was a ghost," she answered, her voice trembling. "A great big one with horrible eyes! It glared at me from the window of the Ship Cottage!"

"Oh, Trixie, you don't really believe that!" George laughed. "There are no ghosts."

61

"Then what was it I saw?" the child demanded. "There's something big with horrible eyes hiding in there!"

Nancy spoke up quietly. "I'll tell you what we'll do, Trixie. You run along to the house with Bess. George and I will go to the music studio and take a look round."

"Maybe that thing will hurt you," the little girl said anxiously.

"We'll be careful. You go with Bess."

Somewhat reluctantly Trixie allowed herself to be led up the path. George and Nancy turned in the opposite direction, walking swiftly to the studio.

"Trixie didn't imagine that she saw glaring eyes watching her," Nancy declared, lowering her voice. "The first day I came here some very strange things happened while I was inside the building. That's why Dad doesn't like me to come here alone."

"You think someone may be hiding there?"

"It's possible. Before Ellen accepts work with Mrs Chatham we must investigate this place thoroughly."

Cautiously the girls circled the quaint little building. They saw no one and heard no unusual sounds.

Nancy tried the door, expecting to walk right in as she had done the first time, but to her surprise it would not open.

"That's odd," she remarked in a puzzled tone. "The studio was unlocked when I was here before."

"Perhaps we can get in through a window," George suggested, testing one on the front of the house.

She could not raise it nor any of the others.

"I wonder if I should ask Mrs Chatham for the key," Nancy mused. Then, answering herself, she said, "Why not? She can only refuse."

The two girls hurried to the main house, where they found Bess seated on the porch with Mrs Chatham. Trixie was playing on the steps with a white cat and laughing shrilly at its antics.

"Can't you please be quiet?" her mother asked irritably.

"You always say that. 'Be quiet; don't do that!' If Daddy were alive, I'd have fun."

"Trixie!" Mrs Chatham shouted. "Not another word or you'll go to your room." The child subsided into silence.

Nancy felt sorry for Trixie, knowing how upset the child had been. She was certain that Mrs Chatham did not know about the unusual happenings at Ship Cottage. To confirm this theory, Nancy casually asked the woman who used the small house.

"Why, no one," Mrs Chatham replied, surprised at the question.

"You never go there yourself?"

"Almost never. I've been reluctant to stir up old memories."

"You keep the studio locked, I suppose?" Nancy inquired.

"Usually I do," Mrs Chatham replied. "For a while I left it unlocked thinking Trixie might like to play there. But she refused to step inside!"

"Did you ever ask her why she dislikes the place so much?"

"It would do no good," Mrs Chatham said. "She has a very vivid imagination and tells outlandish stories."

Nancy was inclined to believe the woman had no idea that Trixie's misbehaviour might result from a feeling of loneliness. If her mother did not believe her and the servants were not kind to her, the child did indeed need a friend. Ellen Smith could be just the person!

"You mentioned the other day that your first husband collected ship models," Nancy remarked after a moment.

"Would you like to see the collection?" Mrs Chatham inquired politely.

"Yes, I would."

"I'll get the key," Mrs Chatham said, rising.

Trixie remained at the house while her mother and the three girls went to the studio. The widow unlocked the front door, pushed it open, and stepped inside. The girls followed.

Nancy's eyes roved about the dusty room. Nothing appeared to have been disturbed since her last visit. There was no sign of either an intruder or an open panel in the wall.

"What charming little ships!" Bess exclaimed as she examined the model of a sailing clipper on the mantel-piece.

While her friends were talking to Mrs Chatham, Nancy seated herself at the piano. Hesitantly she touched the keys. The notes sounded clear and loud, echoing in the room.

"That's certainly strange," she mused.

Turning round, she asked Mrs Chatham if the piano had a secret spring which at times prevented it from being played.

"Goodness, no! Why do you ask?" The woman laughed. But a moment later she said, "It's possible your question may be far more to the point than I first thought. The inventor who lived here might have installed some kind of gadget."

"Then the piano was here when you took over the place?"

"Yes, it was. Nothing has been changed. In fact, this building never has been used."

"You haven't found any secret panels?" Nancy inquired eagerly.

"Not here, but there is one in my bedroom. It serves no real purpose. Once Trixie got behind it by accident, and has never wanted to come into my room since."

Nancy decided to tell Mrs Chatham about her strange experience in the studio. The woman was upset about the man behind the sliding panel. She was greatly relieved when the girls offered to search the movable section in the walls.

"I'll go outside and see how the exterior of the building compares in size with this room," George said.

Bess and Mrs Chatham followed. Nancy resumed her investigating. First she turned up the corner of a rug which lay under the piano. To her surprise she found several wires which evidently ran down one leg of the instrument through the rug and the floor.

"There must be a switch to turn the piano off and on," Nancy mused. "I wonder where it is."

Another search of the walls revealed nothing.

"The switch must be controlled from a spot behind a secret panel!"

Nancy decided to go over each section of the wall reflected in the mirror, moving her hands along the wall an inch at a time. A wooden peg which seemed to secure the wide panel to the sheathing drew her attention. As she fingered it, Nancy felt a slight movement. Between the boards she could see a tiny crack of space.

"I've found the opening!" she thought jubilantly.

Nancy pushed and pulled, increasing the gap only a little at a time. Then suddenly the woodwork gave, sliding back easily. As Nancy turned to shout her discovery, she heard a shrill scream.

"Help! Help! Nancy!"

The cry had come from outside the building. Nancy recognized the voice as George's!

·9·

Shadow of Fear

DARTING from the studio, Nancy spotted George far up the path, pursuing a man whose head was bent low.

Quickly guessing that the fugitive had been caught prowling near the building, Nancy joined in the chase. In a moment she caught up with George, but the two were unable to overtake the fleet-footed man. By the time the girls reached the boundary of the estate, he was out of sight.

"It's no use," George said, halting to catch her breath. "We'll never get him now."

"Did you recognize the man?" Nancy asked. "Was he near the music studio?"

"I'd never seen him before. He just suddenly appeared out of the rear of the building. His head was lowered and I couldn't get a good look at his face."

Before Nancy could question George further, Mrs Chatham and Bess hurried down the path.

"What happened?" Bess asked anxiously. "We heard the cry for help. Did one of you get hurt?"

"No, we're all right," George replied. "After you and Mrs Chatham went off, the man apparently thought no one was here. He pushed aside part of the cottage wall and stepped outside. When he saw me, he took off."

"Goodness!" Bess exclaimed nervously. "There must be a secret passage connected with the studio. That man was probably listening to our conversation when we were inside. He could have harmed us!"

"I found out how to open that secret panel in the studio only a minute ago," Nancy said.

"You did?" Mrs Chatham asked in astonishment.

"I'll show you. But first I want to see the hidden door George found."

George started down the path.

"I'll join you in a minute," Mrs Chatham said, turning in the opposite direction. "I'm going to call the police. It frightens me that someone is prowling about the premises!"

George had no difficulty locating the concealed section. Nancy pushed against the wall and stepped through the narrow opening.

"This passageway must lead along the back wall to an alcove behind the piano," she called, her voice muffled. "Let's explore."

"I'm not as thin as you are, Nancy," Bess complained as she attempted to follow. "I'll never make it!"

"Then go into the studio and enter through the secret panel. I left it open. George and I are bound to meet you somewhere!"

Bess vanished round the building. The other two girls moved along the inner wall until they came to an unlocked door which opened into a small chamber.

"I can't see a thing!" Nancy declared. "We should have brought torches."

"Ouch!" George exclaimed. "This place must be lined with rock!"

Cautiously the girls groped their way towards the

half-open panel ahead. They were glad when Bess
pushed it fully open, allowing light to flood the gloomy
space.

"What did you find?" she called.

"Boxes and lots of other things," Nancy replied,
gazing about her.

"Do you think it's a storage room?" George asked.

"Either that, or some thief's hideaway for loot,"
Nancy commented as she examined a large Chinese
vase.

While the girls were inspecting two trunks, rain
began to patter on the tin roof.

"Just listen to that!" Nancy said in dismay. "And
I wanted to take a look at the footprints near the hidden
door. Perhaps I can beat the storm. George, you stay
inside with Bess. No sense in all of us getting wet."

Hastily Nancy looked about for a board or box lid
to cover the prints but could find neither. She ran
back through the passage and outside. Footprints
made by a man's large shoes were still visible.

The rain descended heavily as Nancy took pencil
and paper from her bag and rapidly drew an outline
of one footmark. The toe of the shoe was very wide,
and the rubber heel had left a peculiar star-design
imprint.

"The marks are nearly washed away now," Nancy
thought ruefully. "But at least I have a sketch."

She closed the secret door and scurried into the
studio. Ten minutes later Mrs Chatham arrived with a
supply of umbrellas, but insisted that the girls stay at
the cottage to see the police. Presently their car pulled
up in front.

The two officers questioned Mrs Chatham and the

girls regarding the trespasser. Unfortunately George's description of him was sketchy. The only tangible clue was the footprint which Nancy had made.

"This should be of some use to us," one of the policemen declared, pocketing the drawing.

Before leaving, the officers inspected the hidden chamber. Mrs Chatham readily identified many of the articles as the property of her first husband. Some she did not recognize but assumed they must have also belonged to him.

After the police had gone, Nancy asked thoughtfully, "Is it possible that Mr Chatham knew of this hiding place and stored goods here without your knowledge?"

"Yes, but I don't see why he wouldn't have told me," Mrs Chatham paused. "Oh, I do hope nothing of John's has been stolen. It would break my heart to lose anything belonging to him."

Tears glistened in her eyes as she lifted a miniature ship, similar to those which the girls had seen in the studio room. For the first time Nancy felt herself warming to Mrs Chatham. No doubt her strange actions resulted from grief and loneliness.

The question that troubled Nancy most was, Who was the mysterious fugitive and was he hiding loot on the premises or taking articles away?

"But how did he learn of this place?" she wondered.

As Nancy mulled over the matter, she absently raised the lid of a leather-covered box. She stared in surprise and delight. Inside, carefully wrapped in tissue paper, were many large, rare sea shells.

"Mrs Chatham, did your first husband collect these?" she asked breathlessly.

"At least I have a sketch of the intruder's footprints,"
Nancy said to herself

"Yes, he did. He loved the sea and everything connected with it."

"You never mentioned your first husband's last name," Nancy said, waiting eagerly for the answer.

"Why, I thought I did. His name was Tomlin—John Tomlin."

"Tomlin!" Nancy could hardly believe her ears. "Then he may be related to Tomlin Smith!" she added, her eyes dancing with excitement.

"Tomlin Smith?" the widow repeated. "Who is he, may I ask?"

"Ellen's father! Mrs Chatham, do you have a photograph of John Tomlin?"

"Unfortunately, no."

Nancy revealed everything she knew about Mr Smith's request for his missing twin brother but did not mention the map. She also related the story she had heard from Bill Tomlin's father.

"My husband had a fine baritone voice," Mrs Chatham declared. "He loved songs of the sea and collected them."

"Everything tallies with the information given me by Bill Tomlin's father! Without question your first husband was related to the Tomlin family in Kirkland. The two men were cousins. Now if only I can prove a relationship to Tomlin Smith! Did your husband have a middle name?"

"If so, he didn't mention it. At no time did my husband tell me much about his early life," Mrs. Chatham added.

"He never spoke of his father?" Nancy asked, fingering a large pink shell.

"No. You see, we were married after knowing each

other only a few weeks. John settled me in a lovely little cottage, furnished it beautifully, and then set sail but he did not return."

"Was his ship lost?" Bess inquired sympathetically.

"My husband was taken ill and died on a voyage to Japan," Mrs Chatham explained, her eyes misty.

The widow revealed a few additional facts but none of great value. Her husband, she said, had been ten years older than she and frequently had spoken of himself as a "son of the sea."

"That might mean his father had been a captain too," Nancy mused. "Tell me, Mrs Chatham, did your first husband leave any papers or letters?"

"Several boxes were brought to me some time after his death. I received a small amount of money and an insurance policy. I'll confess I read very few of the letters, for they seemed to be old business ones and I wasn't interested. I was too heartbroken to care. But I saved every one of them. They should be somewhere in this studio. I asked Mr Chatham to bring them here."

"I'll look right—"

At that instant a fearful shriek cut the air. The group was electrified for an instant, then Nancy made a dash outside.

"*Moth-er!*" came in terrified tones from somewhere to the right.

"Trixie!"

Nancy dashed off with Mrs Chatham, Bess and George close on her heels.

"Where are you?" the child's mother called.

There was no answer!

Frantically the group ran to left and to right,

shouting Trixie's name. Suddenly a muffled sound reached Nancy's ears. She stopped short to listen.

The child was crying and saying, "I want to get out! I want to get out!"

Almost directly in front of her Nancy saw a yawning hole in the ground. She peered down. Indistinctly she could see a figure.

"Trixie!" Nancy gasped. "Are you hurt?"

"I'm okay. Where's my m-mother?" came the sobbing voice from below. "Please h-help me out!"

The child had fallen into a dry well hole.

Nancy lay down on the ground and stretched one arm into the chasm. She could not reach Trixie.

"I'll get a ladder," Nancy said reassuringly. "Don't be frightened."

By this time the others had come up. Mrs Chatham, hearing that her daughter was unharmed, alternately laughed and cried. In a few minutes George located the gardener and he brought a long ladder.

"I want Nancy Drew to come down," called Trixie as the man started to descend.

"Nancy, do you mind?" Mrs Chatham asked.

"Not at all."

As Nancy began the climb, the woman snapped at the gardener, "Hoskins, how do you account for this uncovered hole? You are supposed to have charge of the grounds."

"Mrs Chatham, I had no idea this hole was here. Probably it was overgrown and—"

Nancy heard no more for she had reached the bottom rung. Trixie, her knees slightly scratched, impulsively hugged her rescuer and scrambled up the ladder. Nancy quickly glanced about. To her right was an opening to a tunnel. The young sleuth wanted to investigate it but decided that right now she had better hurry to the top of the well. Mrs Chatham stood there hugging her daughter.

Nancy said mysteriously to Bess and George, "Very interesting place down there. I'll be back in a minute." She headed for her car. When Nancy returned, she held her flashlight.

Bess shook her head. "Don't tell me you've found something in that hole!"

"Uh-huh. Want to come along?"

"George, you go," Bess shivered in reply.

Excited over this latest development, George followed her friend into the dark pit. Nancy swung the beam of her light around the opening of the cavern. It was fairly wide and about six feet high. Cautiously the girls walked in for several feet to a point where the tunnel turned abruptly. As Nancy's light exposed the cavern beyond, they stared open-mouthed. Across one wall and on the ceiling flickered the shadow of a weird, forbidding shape.

· 10 ·

Valuable Property

THE flashlight focused on a large dugout beneath the silhouette. In the centre stood a strange-looking contraption, rusted and crumbling with age.

George broke the silence. "It has dials. Looks like an old oil burner."

Nancy did not reply. She pointed to an envelope attached to the unweildy object. Printed on the envelope was a warning:

HIGHLY EXPLOSIVE
DO NOT TOUCH

"In that case," George put in quickly, "let's get out of here."

Nancy tugged her friend back, saying, "Wait a minute. You don't really believe this thing will explode, do you? Obviously it has been here a long while and—"

"*Mm*," George murmured warily. "Nevertheless it could go off."

She gulped as Nancy beamed the light through a decayed section, then said, "Well, Miss Detective, what next?"

"Two things. First, I've been wondering how the machine got here. I thought there might have been a door connecting this tunnel with the main house. But since there is none, the machine must have been constructed in this dugout," Nancy declared. "The only person who would have master-minded such a project was Silas Norse."

"I agree," said George. "What's the second thing?"

"The envelope."

Carefully Nancy removed the dusty envelope from the mechanism and opened it. A letter inside was headed: *List of Inventions in House and Grounds of Rocky Edge.* About ten were mentioned, revealing all kinds of strange gadgets secreted on the place, including the secret panel and piano in the music studio.

At the bottom was a description of Norse's machine, which he called his "greatest achievement." Many of the words were in German and the girls understood little of it. But the last line read:

" 'In this spot it has harmed no one yet.' "

Nancy stopped abruptly, saying, "There's a break here in this note with a short pencilled sentence. 'It will never harm anyone. I cannot finish my work. I am too ill. Silas Norse.' "

"We'd better tell Mrs Chatham about all of this," George urged. "She'll want to have this machine dismantled completely and see that all the other gadgets are removed for the safety of Trixie, herself, and the people who work on the estate."

Nancy agreed. As the two started towards the ladder, she said, "One thing I want to do right away. Advise her to take Trixie away from here until the place has had a thorough investigation."

When the girls emerged, Bess was waiting for them. "You must have found a gold mine," she said, adding almost immediately, "Mrs Chatham took Trixie back to the house, but said she'd return to the studio alone."

"Shall we go there?" Nancy suggested. "We'll tell you and Mrs Chatham what we found."

After Nancy had located the gardener and made sure that he covered the hole with heavy planks, the trio headed for Ship Cottage. Mrs Chatham was busy searching through some boxes which she had carried from the windowless secret chamber into the main room.

"Nancy and George stumbled upon something unusual in the well," Bess told her.

Nancy related the whole story and produced the inventor's letter.

Mrs Chatham was both surprised and alarmed. "I never dreamed such things were here!" she exclaimed. "If I had known, I wouldn't have stayed."

This was Nancy's chance to make a suggestion. "Until Rocky Edge can be thoroughly searched, don't you think it might be wise to take Trixie away on a holiday?"

"You're right. I wish we could go somewhere far away," Mrs Chatham replied. "But I detest travelling by car. And planes—well, I think the most relaxing way to travel is by boat."

Nancy had not intended to tell Mrs Chatham about the treasure map in Tomlin Smith's possession until the relationship between him and the woman's first husband was established. Suddenly it occurred to her that should this be the case, Mrs Chatham might propose an expedition to the mysterious island.

"Would you enjoy a trip to a treasure island?" she inquired with a smile.

"Are you joking?" the woman asked.

When Nancy had finished the amazing tale of the Tomlin twins' inheritance, Mrs Chatham declared with enthusiasm, "If the missing half of the map can be found, I'll finance the entire trip. Nothing would please me more than to have you, Bess, George, and Ellen join us."

Bess's eyes popped at the generous invitation and she and George thanked the widow.

Nancy said, "Ellen will be thrilled! At the first opportunity I'll tell the Smith family the wonderful news." Then she added ruefully, "Finding the map is our only problem—"

"I just remembered," Mrs Chatham interrupted, "that John did say we might go treasure hunting together. At the time I'm afraid I really didn't take the idea very seriously."

Nancy said eagerly, "That almost proves the relationship of the two Tomlins! And if that's so, then your husband must have had the missing portion of the map. Maybe it's—"

"In the box of papers I've been looking for!" Mrs Chatham finished excitedly. "This detective work is new to me, but I'm trying to catch on."

Suddenly Nancy disappeared into the dark chamber.

Mrs Chatham called after her, "Oh, Nancy, I've been all through there. I'm sure the box is gone. Maybe it was stolen."

But the young detective was unwilling to give up. She beamed her torch into the corners of the narrow room. Bess and George watched from the panel entrance.

Finaly Nancy stooped to move a pile of small oriental rugs. "What's this?" she murmured.

Against the wall where the carpets had lain was a rectangle of wood which did not match the adjoining panels. As Nancy pushed against it, the section opened inwards, revealing a small, dark recess.

"Another secret hiding place!" she called out.

Her two friends dashed to Nancy's side, Mrs Chatham at their heels. With mounting excitement, Nancy thrust her arm into the opening.

"I've found something!" she cried out, and a moment later brought out a tin box.

"That's it!" Mrs Chatham exclaimed. "That's the missing box!"

As Nancy unfastened the lid, she hoped they had at last found the long-lost half of the map. But the metal box contained only two objects—a small key and a bank book. The name of the depositor was John Tomlin. Nancy had hoped it would be John Abner Tomlin. The bank was in New Kirk, a seacoast city, and there was a large sum of money on deposit.

"No doubt this key unlocks his safe-deposit box in the same bank," George put in.

"I must go to New Kirk at once," the widow declared.

Nancy spoke up. "You may have some trouble at the bank. You'll probably need proper identification and notarized papers. Why not discuss the situation first with my dad?"

"Yes, yes. I mustn't lose my head."

When Mrs Chatham had calmed down sufficiently, Bess observed, "I've been wondering about this recess in the wall. I don't recall that it was included in Silas Norse's list of places where his inventions were."

"It wasn't," Nancy confirmed, "but that doesn't necessarily mean Mr Norse did *not* put it in. From the appearance of his weak handwriting, indicating poor health, I doubt that he made a record of all his work.

"I do have another idea, though," she went on. "Perhaps the man that George spied coming out of the concealed opening knows about the missing map!"

"What!" her listeners chorused.

"It's only a hunch but he may have stolen it from this box. Furthermore, he must have hidden the box here, not Mr Chatham. Obviously Mr Chatham did not know the contents of this box. If he had, he certainly would have told his wife."

Nancy's conclusions stunned Mrs Chatham.

George tried to comfort her by saying, "We're used to Nancy's whizz-bang brain. I suppose, Nancy, you can tell us the thief's name, too." She grinned.

Nancy laughed. With a twinkle in her eye, she replied, "I might make a guess. I'll bet he's Spike Doty!"

She told of the old newspaper account of how Spike Doty, the burglar at Norse's mansion, had sued the inventor. She also mentioned that the police had deduced from her drawing and description that the thief at Ellen's home was Spike.

Before anyone could comment, Trixie came to the doorway of the studio. "Mother!" she called loudly. "There's a man and a woman at the house. They want to talk to you."

"Did they give you their names?" Mrs Chatham asked.

When Trixie shook her head, the widow excused herself and went quickly to the house. Her daughter did not follow. Instead Trixie entered the cottage and peeked into the secret chamber where papers and objects had been carefully sorted. To keep the child from touching the articles, Nancy diverted her attention by saying:

"How would you like to play a magic piano?"

"A magic piano?" Trixie repeated, her eyes opening wide. "Where is it?"

"Here in the studio." She led the little girl to the instrument.

After Trixie had seated herself and played a few notes, Nancy turned off the control switch. Silence.

The child laughed. "How do you do it? Show me, please!"

Nancy smiled at the word "please," so different from Trixie's usual manner. As Nancy was showing her ɔw to operate the switch, Mrs Chatham reappeared.

"Nancy, I'd like you to come to the house and meet Mr and Mrs Brown. They have an interesting story which may shed some light on the matter of the missing map."

Excitedly Nancy followed Mrs Chatham up the winding path. A car Nancy did not recognize stood in the driveway. Mr and Mrs Brown sat on the porch.

The couple stared in astonishment as Nancy approached. The man said something to his companion, then both dashed from the porch and into the car.

"Well, what do you think of that!" Mrs Chatham exclaimed indignantly.

Nancy had sprinted towards the man, but he was too quick for her. Before she could reach the car, it sped down the driveway.

"Why did they run away?" Mrs Chatham asked puzzled.

"Because," Nancy announced, "they are the couple who kidnapped me from Emerson College!"

· 11 ·

Clue to a Treasure

THE car had pulled away so swiftly that Nancy barely had time to jot down its licence number. She ran into the house to call the police, thinking a patrol car might be able to capture the kidnappers.

With Mrs Chatham hovering at her side, Nancy quickly reported what had happened, then hung up the phone. She turned to the widow.

"Please tell me what you know about the Browns."

"They introduced themselves as Mr and Mrs Fred Brown, and said they were trying to find the widow of Captain John Tomlin. They claimed to have known him well before his death."

"Did they question you about the map?" Nancy asked.

"They hinted that Captain Tomlin had told them a great secret before his death and warned me to be on my guard if I were his widow."

"On guard?"

"It seems that an unscrupulous man—they wouldn't give his name—is determined to get hold of a valuable paper belonging to my first husband."

"Of course they meant the map!"

"I thought so but pretended otherwise. The Browns advised me to leave Rocky Edge before the man

84

might threaten or harm me. I told them I wanted a friend to hear their story before I made any decision. I didn't mention your name."

"My sudden appearance must have given them a great shock," Nancy commented.

"I wonder how much they really know about the lost map," Mrs Chatham said.

"Probably not much. They may believe you have it here. Either they're working with that man who hid in the studio, or else they hope to outwit him and get it themselves."

Mrs Chatham walked nervously to the French window and gazed into the garden.

Nancy said, "I suggest you hire guards. The Browns may sneak back and search for the map."

Mrs Chatham promised to attend to the matter directly.

"Do you feel we should give up the proposed trip to New Kirk?" the widow asked as she walked with Nancy to the convertible.

Nancy replied quickly, "Considering what has happened, I think it's very important to learn the contents of your husband's safe-deposit box."

"Then I'll see your father as soon as I can." Mrs Chatham declared.

After saying goodbye, Nancy picked up Bess and George and said she wanted to go home via Wayland and stop at the police station.

"I'd like to talk to the chief, but not on the phone from here. Mrs Chatham is too upset."

Nancy told the girls about the mysterious couple who had come to call and finished just as she reached the police station. There was no news of the Browns, but the chief confirmed Nancy's suspicion that the one clear footprint recently made by the intruder at the Rocky Edge studio belonged to Spike Doty.

"Spike first appeared locally while a seaman on a river steamer. After a prison sentence for burglary he was released and went to New York. We lost track of him. But we'll keep looking for Spike and the Browns, too."

On the way back Bess and George picked up their car. When Nancy reached home she found a special-delivery envelope from Bill Tomlin's father. He had enclosed the faded photograph of a man about thirty dressed in a sea captain's uniform.

"What a good clue!" she thought. "I must show this to Mr Smith and Mrs Chatham."

Nancy gave her father an account of her recent adventures, describing her abduction by the Browns and their unexpected appearance at Rocky Edge. She ended by asking permission to accompany Mrs Chatham to New Kirk.

"You may go, but only on the condition that I talk to Mrs Chatham first," the lawyer replied.

That evening Nancy mulled over the strange developments in the case. "Where do the Browns and Spike and Rorke fit into the picture?" she pondered. "Are they working together or separately?"

When Nancy finally went to bed she dreamed of a heavy-set man with evil eyes peering at her from behind various objects. In this fantasy she seemed to be standing on a high revolving platform. Regardless of which direction it turned, she kept seeing the same terrifying man in different costumes. Nancy awoke and sat up.

"What a nightmare! I can see that face yet!"

She realized that her mind had played a trick on her. The face in her dreams was that of the man on the ladder at the Smith home. The cruel, beady eyes and bearded face were those of the "apparition" which had haunted the Ship Cottage at Rocky Edge.

"Why, that's a clue!" she thought suddenly. "Why didn't I think of asking Trixie before?"

Leaping from her bed, Nancy ran to her desk and switched on a light. She seized a crayon and sketched the leering face she had seen in her dream.

"Now I have two pictures to show," she thought, "the photo to Mrs Chatham and this sketch to her daughter. Trixie's identification would be double proof that Spike Doty is the ghost of Ship Cottage."

Nancy's opportunity came the next morning. The widow phoned that she and Trixie would call on Carson Drew at his office. Nancy said she would be there too.

She at once showed the faded photograph to Mrs Chatham, who quickly recognized the captain as her first husband. "Yes, that's John. Of course he looks younger than the way I knew him."

Nancy said she would show the photograph to Tomlin Smith on her next visit. She then offered to take care of Trixie while Mrs Chatham and Mr Drew talked. Nancy led the child to an ante-room and took the crayon sketch from her handbag.

"I have a picture to show you," Nancy said. "This is a drawing I made last night."

The child gave a muffled shriek!

"It's the same ghost!" she cried. "Take it away, please! Even the picture scares me!"

Nancy hugged the little girl and spoke soothingly to her. In a moment Trixie's fears were gone. Soon Mrs Chatham and Mr Drew came out of his private office.

"Everything is arranged," the widow declared happily as she turned to Nancy. "Your father prepared the papers I'll need in New Kirk and made an appointment with the bank's president. Nancy, you're to go with me."

"Wonderful!" Nancy exclaimed, flashing her father a grateful glance. "When do we leave?"

"In two hours, if you can be ready."

"I can be ready in fifteen minutes," Nancy laughed. "How about plane reservations?"

"I made them by phone," Mr Drew put in.

"Did you hire guards to watch your house?" Nancy asked Mrs Chatham.

"Yes, two men are there."

Nancy looked at Trixie, then drew the woman aside. "Perhaps Ellen Smith could come to your house and take care of Trixie while we're away."

Mrs Chatham was pleased at the suggestion. Fortunately Nancy was able to reach Ellen by phone. She said she would gladly stay with Trixie. Ellen could barely contain her excitement when told of Mrs Chatham's generous invitation to go on a cruise in search of the treasure island.

Then she said, "About Trixie, I'll have to leave tomorrow afternoon."

"We'll be back by that time," Nancy replied, then hung up. "Mrs Chatham, it's all arranged."

The grateful woman relayed the news to Trixie, who was delighted.

After the Chathams had gone, Mr Drew turned to

his daughter. "Besides Ellen, have you told anyone else about going to New Kirk?" he asked.

"I discussed it with Hannah. That's all."

Mr Drew nodded approval. "I've advised Mrs Chatham to keep the reason for her trip a secret."

"You think someone may follow us?"

"I doubt that, but it's better to be cautious," her father said. "The Browns have demonstrated their intense interest in the map, Nancy. That's why I want you to be careful."

"I will, Dad. And now I have something for you."

She handed him the crayon sketch of the Ship Cottage "ghost" and told him of Trixie's positive identification.

"I'll tell the police," he offered, studying the face. "I hope Trixie was sure and not just frightened by the sinister-looking face."

"She is very bright," Nancy replied. "I believe we can depend on her. Well, I must hurry to catch the plane!"

Aided by Mrs. Gruen, Nancy quickly packed an overnight bag and changed into travelling clothes. A short time later she and Mrs Chatham were winging towards New Kirk. At the end of a speedy but un-eventful trip, they checked into a hotel and then proceeded to the bank.

No sooner had they entered than Mrs Chatham began to display signs of nervousness. While she and Nancy waited to see the president, the widow fingered the legal papers Mr Drew had given her.

"Now what was it your father told me to say?" she asked in panic. In the same breath she continued, "Won't you do the talking, Nancy?"

"I'll be glad to if you wish, Mrs Chatham."

Nancy had only a few minutes to glance over the material before she and Mrs Chatham were ushered into the private office of Mr Dowell, the president. Nancy made a simple presentation of the case, offering proof of Mrs Chatham's identity. She also gave the man a letter requesting the opening of Captain John Tomlin's safe-deposit box.

"For a long time we've tried to locate Captain Tomlin or his heirs," Mr Dowell said. "Rentals on the box have accumulated, you know."

"I'll be glad to pay whatever amount is due the bank," Mrs Chatham said. "May we look at the contents today?"

"I fear that will be impossible," the banker answered. "However, if we find your papers in good order, it's possible the box can be opened tomorrow in the presence of someone from the surrogate's office."

After making an appointment for nine o'clock the following day, Nancy and Mrs Chatham returned to the hotel. Despite their disappointment, the two thoroughly enjoyed the evening at a fine restaurant.

At bedtime Nancy was summoned to the telephone. Mrs Chatham, who had been calling her home, said Ellen Smith wished to speak to her.

"Oh, Nancy," Ellen said in a strained voice, "please don't stay away any longer than you have to. I didn't want to frighten Mrs Chatham, but her place is terribly spooky, with creepy shadows in the garden. Twice I've called to the guards but no one answered. I don't believe they're even on duty."

For the sake of Mrs Chatham, Nancy kept calm. "Ellen, why don't you ask Hannah Gruen to come over? Dad has to be away tonight and tomorrow, I know, so she's alone. Please do that."

The girl promised, relief in her voice. Nancy went to bed but found it hard to sleep and was awake early. She hoped Mrs Chatham's business could be attended to at once and an early return made to River Heights. When the two reached the bank, Mr Dowell greeted them cordially and presented an official from the surrogate's office.

"The box will be opened without further delay," he assured them. "I've arranged for an inheritance tax man to be here this morning. He'll list the contents for tax purposes."

He personally conducted Nancy and Mrs Chatham to an underground room and sat at one end of a long table.

The tax official directed Nancy and Mrs Chatham to sit at the far end of the table. Then he and the bank official sat down with the box before them. As the government man raised the lid, the bulky papers that filled the box crackled. He picked up the top envelope and exclaimed, "Hm! What's this? . . . 'Clue to a Treasure'!"

·12·

Triple Alarm

"THAT must be it," Nancy thought, trying to control her mounting excitement. She and Mrs Chatham exchanged looks of apprehension. They hoped the official would not ask questions about the treasure. Both were quickly relieved when the men merely glanced at the enclosed sheet, put it back, and went on to examine the rest of the papers. Finally the contents were listed. Nothing was taxable. At length Mrs Chatham and Nancy were left alone.

"Thank goodness!" Mrs Chatham murmured in relief. "Now we can look in that envelope. Surely it must contain the missing map."

With trembling fingers she took out the contents.

"It's a letter," she said, unable to hide her disappointment.

"Is it signed bv Captain Tomlin?" Nancy asked.

"Yes, this is hi ndwriting."

Did the letter tell what became of the missing treasure map? Nancy wondered.

Her voice vibrant with emotion, Mrs Chatham read the entire note aloud. In it her husband revealed details of his early life never before disclosed to her, including the fact that he had dropped the name Abner because he did not like it. There were other facts sufficient to prove that he and Tomlin Smith were twin brothers.

"So that part of the mystery is solved!" said Nancy.

The letter concerned itself mainly with the inheritance originally secreted by Captain Tomlin's seafaring grandfather.

"Listen to this!" Mrs Chatham exclaimed as she came to a particularly significant paragraph.

" 'All these years I have kept the torn section of a treasure map given me by my father. Fearing theft I made a copy of it. Only a month ago, this very copy was stolen from my cabin, unquestionably by a member of the crew.' "

"What is the date of the letter?" Nancy asked as the widow paused to catch her breath.

"It was written only a week before my husband's death. He continues:

" 'I have taken the original map and hidden it on the *Warwick*. This map, if combined with the section in the possession of my missing twin brother, will lead to the discovery of our grandfather's great treasure.' "

"That doesn't add up!" Nancy exclaimed. "Wasn't the *Warwick* the name of the vessel your husband sailed?"

"You're right, Nancy, it was."

"Then how could he have removed the parchment map from his own ship and still have hidden it there?"

"Perhaps he meant he hid it somewhere in another part of the vessel—away from his cabin," Mrs Chatham suggested.

"That doesn't seem likely," Nancy said, shaking her head. "No, I'm sure Captain Tomlin would never have risked having the original found by members of his crew. Especially after the copy had been stolen."

Mrs Chatham furrowed her brow in bewilderment as Nancy went on, "Apparently he thought you would understand where the map was hidden."

"I haven't the faintest idea!"

Nancy was silent for several moments as she re-read the letter. Then suddenly her face brightened.

"I get it!" she exclaimed. "Captain Tomlin owned the ship models you have at the studio on Rocky Edge, didn't he?"

"Yes. He had many of them custom-built."

"And they were sent to you from the ship after his death?"

"Yes."

"Among the collection was there a replica of the *Warwick*?"

"Oh dear! I can't remember," Mrs Chatham said. "There were so many of the little boats. I sold a few of them."

Nancy was worried. Mrs Chatham might have sold the *Warwick*!

"You think my husband hid his half of the map in a model of the *Warwick*?" the widow asked.

"Doesn't that seem reasonable?" Nancy replied.

"Oh, it does!" the woman cried in despair. "And to think I may have disposed of it unwittingly! I'll have no peace of mind until we find out. We'll take the first plane home," Mrs Chatham decided instantly.

The two were soon en route to River Heights. Aided by a strong tail wind, their plane arrived ahead of schedule.

They hailed a taxi and rode to Rocky Edge. As the

cab rolled through the open gate, Nancy observed that no guards were on duty.

"Shouldn't at least one of the special detectives be stationed at the gate?" she inquired.

"They aren't detectives," Mrs Chatham replied. "My gardener knew two strong men who were out of work, so we gave them the job. I'm sure they're around here somewhere."

Shortly the taxi pulled up in front of the main house. As Nancy and Mrs Chatham stepped out, a servant rushed up to them.

"Oh, Mrs Chatham," the young woman said, puffing, "what are we going to do? What are we going to do?" she repeated hurriedly. "I'm so sorry, so very sorry."

The widow put a comforting arm around the girl's shoulders and tried to remain calm. "Now tell me what the problem is," she said. "No one's had an accident I hope."

"No, no," came the sobbing reply.

Mrs Chatham's face grew stern. "Well, then tell me what's going on," she said, raising her voice abruptly.

"Trixie is missing!"

"What!"

"Your daughter is missing. We can't find her anywhere."

The words ringing loudly in her ears, Mrs Chatham made no response. She stumbled up the porch steps to a chair.

Nancy had been silent, not wishing to interrupt the woman's conversation with her employee. But now she inquired if Ellen Smith and Hannah Gruen had left.

Tears trickled down the young woman's face. She

answered. "They both went away right after lunch. Miss Smith had to leave because of a singing lesson. And your housekeeper, Miss Drew, left because she couldn't get anything to eat. The cook resented her being here and wouldn't even make her a sandwich, much less let her into the kitchen to make her own meal.

"Where are the guards?" Nancy asked.

"Oh, they got better jobs, so they left."

Nancy coaxed the girl to tell as much as she could about Trixie's disappearance.

"She's been gone close to two hours," was the reply.

Mrs Chatham spoke up. "Have you searched everywhere? Over the cliff—and down by the river?"

"Yes, Madam, everywhere."

Mrs Chatham seemed relieved by this statement. "Then Trixie has run away! Well, this isn't the first time. She'll come home."

"I don't wish to alarm you, Mrs Chatham," said Nancy, "but I'm afraid she may have been kidnapped."

The widow gasped. "Then we must call the police at once!"

As the child's mother started towards the house, Nancy followed closely. When they entered the hall both noticed a sheet of paper lying near the telephone.

"What's this?" Mrs Chatham asked, picking it up.

At a glance she saw that it was a ransom note. Written in a bold scrawl was the alarming message:

If you want to see your kid again have this amount ready when our messenger arrives. Do not notify the police or you'll be sorry.

At the bottom of the paper was a request for thousands of dollars.

"Oh, no!" Mrs Chatham groaned.

For a moment Nancy thought the woman was going to faint but she managed to steady herself and sat down.

"I don't want to pay the money," Mrs Chatham stated, then said, "But what will happen to Trixie if I refuse?"

"Please don't worry about that—at least not yet," Nancy said, studying the ransom note again. "The kidnapping could be an inside job."

"I don't agree with you," Mrs Chatham returned with conviction. "While my servants may be careless, they're all honest. Whoever left this note here did so without the knowledge of my employees."

Nancy tactfully withheld her own opinion.

"I think I should call the police," Mrs. Chatham said nervously.

"Please wait until we've had an opportunity to search the grounds thoroughly," Nancy advised. "I have an idea."

Without explaining her hunch, Nancy hurried from the house. She ran down the path, a question burning in her brain. *Was Trixie a prisoner somewhere on the estate?* Perhaps in Ship Cottage with its secret room and sliding panels?

Cautiously Nancy opened the door of the music studio and peered inside. The room was vacant, but on a chair lay a child's hair ribbon.

Nancy groped for the peg which opened the secret panel. As the wall slid back slowly she was almost certain she heard a movement in the dark chamber.

"Trix—" she started to call.

At the same moment a hard object struck Nancy and she blacked out.

Q.M.M.   D

· 13 ·

Tracing the Warwick

WHEN Nancy Drew opened her eyes, the room was spinning. A little girl, her mouth gagged with a white handkerchief, was staring down at her.

"Trixie!" Nancy murmured weakly and slowly got to her feet.

She removed the handkerchief and the child began to sob. "Oh, I didn't mean to hit you!"

"*You* hit me? But why—and how?"

In bewilderment Nancy looked at the cords binding the child's ankles and hands which were crossed in front of her. She unknotted them as Trixie answered:

"I thought you were that awful man coming back. So when you opened the panel, I knocked this big stick off the shelf. It fell on top of you."

She pointed to a croquet mallet lying on the floor.

"Trixie, who put you in here? Tell me quickly."

"That horrid ghost you drew a picture of!"

"And he brought you to the cottage?"

"No, I came by myself," Trixie admitted. "I didn't think the ghost would bother me when the guards were around."

"How did you get in?"

"With the key. I saw where my mother put it after she locked up the place."

98

"Then what happened?"

"I was playing the piano when that bad man—the ghost—grabbed me. I couldn't yell 'cause he put his hand over my mouth. He tied me up and carried me in here."

She gulped and started to cry again but Nancy gave her a comforting hug. Hand in hand they walked back to the house. Mrs Chatham was so relieved to see her daughter she barely listened to Nancy's explanation of what had happened to Trixie.

When the excitement had subsided, Nancy mentioned the ransom note. "I wonder why the messenger hasn't come yet. I should think the kidnappers wouldn't lose any time sending someone over here, Mrs Chatham."

"You're right, Nancy. I'll call the police right away so they can capture him."

"Perhaps," Nancy said, "the man has been here and already left."

Seeing the woman's confused expression, she explained, "Whoever was sent to get the money from you may have spotted Trixie and me outside, and knew the game was up. Please don't worry any more, Mrs Chatham. Get a good night's rest and in the morning, if it's all right, I'd like to resume the search for Captain Tomlin's map."

Police were stationed at the house and the cottage. In the morning they reported to Nancy, who had stayed overnight, that no one had shown up.

She and Mrs Chatham went to the studio to examine the various ship models. Each bore a small brass plate with a name engraved on it, but the *Warwick* was not there. Moreover, a thorough examination of the miniature ships did not reveal a single hiding place.

"Mrs Chatham, how many did you sell?" Nancy asked.

"About ten or twelve," the woman said. "I listed the purchasers."

"You did?" Nancy cried, her spirits reviving. "And the names of each model?"

"I don't remember about that. Perhaps I can find the record book."

Mrs Chatham returned to the main house, and within minutes came back with a small black book.

"Apparently I didn't write down the names of the ship models," she said, glancing through the book. "Only the prices paid and the eleven purchasers."

"Was Captain Tomlin's vessel very well known?" Nancy asked.

"No. It was a small ship and rather old."

"Then a model of it would be less likely to command a high price. I'm tempted to start our investigation with the purchasers of the least expensive ones."

They noted that a man named J. K. Trumbull had paid the lowest price. His address was given as Hope, a small city about twenty-five miles away. But to Nancy's disappointment his telephone number was not listed in the directory.

"I'll have to drive there and try to find Mr Trumbull," she declared. "Maybe Bess and George will go with me."

When the girls were informed of the trip, both were eager to accompany Nancy. The cousins packed a picnic lunch and were waiting when she drove up in front of the Marvin residence.

Within an hour the trio arrived in Hope and began

making inquiries about J. K. Trumbull. A local shopkeeper finally directed them to a small white house. Its owner was a short, curly-haired man.

Introductions were exchanged and Nancy asked, "Mr Trumbull, I understand you purchased a model of the ship *Warwick*. Is that correct?"

"Yes." He paused. "Say, are you the one who advertised in the paper saying a good price would be paid for the *Warwick?*"

"Why, no," Nancy replied, surprised.

"Do you still have that paper?" George asked the man quickly. "And was there a name signed to the ad?"

"No, I threw it away days ago," he asnwered. "To your second question, there was no name, just a box number. I didn't need to know it because I have no intention of selling the model."

The girls' hearts sank at Mr Trumbull's statement. Nancy explained that they were trying to recover the model of the *Warwick* for Mrs Chatham, whose first husband had sailed the original vessel.

"May we borrow the model?" she asked. "We believe it contains a clue which may help solve a mystery for Mrs Chatham."

"What sort of clue?" Mr Trumbull inquired, his interest aroused.

"I can't tell you, for I'm not sure myself."

He remained silent for a moment, studying the girls. Then, to their relief, he smiled broadly.

"I thought you just wanted the little *Warwick* to sell at a profit. Now that I see otherwise, you may have the ship for exactly what I paid."

Nancy gratefully gave him the sum. With her two

friends she delightedly carried the model to the car.

"We'll drive out of town and then examine the model," she proposed.

Unnoticed by the girls, a car which had been parked across the street followed only a short distance behind. The occupants had observed the three leave the Trumbull house with the *Warwick*.

"Nancy Drew would never buy a ship model unless it has something to do with the parchment map!" the woman was saying to her husband. "If only we can get our hands on it! I'll bet it's the *Warwick!*"

"I have a feeling this is going to be our lucky day," the man replied. "The advertising trick didn't work, but now we have Nancy Drew and the *Warwick* right where we want 'em!"

"Please be careful, Fred. Nancy has preferred a kidnapping charge against us and—"

"Listen, Irene, you worry too much," he retorted as he speeded up to keep Nancy's car in sight.

With no suspicion that they were being followed, the girls pulled into a shady lane. While Bess took the picnic hamper, Nancy and George examined the *Warwick*.

"If the map isn't in here, I'll be very disappointed," Nancy declared, her fingers exploring the ship's hull. "It must be, unless Captain Tomlin's letter meant something totally different."

"Can't you find it, Nancy?" George asked, with growing impatience. Bess, silent, anxiously fastened her eyes on the little ship.

While the search was in progress, Fred Brown parked his car some distance away. Noiselessly he stole among the trees until he was directly behind Nancy's convertible. He listened closely to the girls' excited conversation.

"Look at this!" he heard Nancy exclaim. "A tiny door in the bottom of the ship!"

"Try it!" George urged.

"I can't seem to get it open," Nancy answered. There was a short pause, then she cried, "It's coming now! I feel something inside!"

"Is it the map?" Bess asked tremulously. "Is it, Nancy?" -

"I'm not sure yet. Yes, it is! Or a copy of it. We've found the missing directions!"

The eavesdropper, still crouched behind the car, smiled with satisfaction. He nodded with even deeper satisfaction as he heard Bess suggest to Nancy that she replace the half map in the ship, so that they could eat their picnic lunch.

Nancy did not reply. She was thinking, "I wish we could start on that cruise right away!"

Bess exclaimed, "This excitement has given me a big appetite!"

"Let's carry the hamper over to a shady spot in the woods," George added, pointing. "It's too sunny here."

"There doesn't seem to be anyone around," Nancy said. "I suppose the ship will be safe in the car." She looked about, then set the model on the front seat. Picking up a Thermos jug, she added, "Bess, please lock the car."

"Sure thing."

Fred Brown quickly ducked behind a clump of bushes, spreading their leaves, to watch Bess's movements. She had trouble with one of the snap locks and called out to Nancy. But by now the other two girls had disappeared into the woods and did not hear her. She looked at the little ship.

"I'm sure it'll be safe," Bess told herself, and started off to join the others.

As soon as she was out of sight, Fred Brown crept from his hiding place. He stole around the car, opened the front door, and snatched the precious *Warwick!*

· 14 ·

Sneak Attack

In the meantime Nancy and her friends were enjoying the picnic lunch under the trees. Bess had reported the faulty lock on the car door.

"I'll have to get it fixed," Nancy said, then smiled. "Don't worry, Bess. There surely aren't any thieves in this lovely place."

Bess reached for a second helping of potato salad. "Isn't it wonderful! We've found the map and it may lead to buried treasure!"

"Providing Mrs Chatham doesn't change her mind about financing the trip," George reminded her cousin. "What do you think, Nancy? Will she go through with it?"

"Oh, Mrs Chatham is very enthusiastic. If we succeed in piecing the map together, she promised to ask both of you, and also Burt and Dave if you like," Nancy added with a twinkle in her eyes. "And Ned, Ellen, and Bill Tomlin."

"Terrific!" Bess exclaimed gleefully. "Four couples. What a houseparty!"

"Four couples and Trixie," said Nancy.

It was growing late, so after Bess had consumed the last sandwich, the girls gathered up the picnic debris and returned to the car.

"I'd like to look at that map again," George remarked.

Bess, who was a few steps ahead, swung open the car door. She gasped in astonishment at the empty seat.

"Oh, no! We shouldn't have left the ship model in here!" she wailed.

"What's happened?" Nancy asked.

"Someone stole it while we were eating!" Bess exclaimed. "Nancy, will you ever forgive me?"

George eyed her cousin disapprovingly. "Think of all the hours we spent trying to find that map."

Nancy gazed carefully about the clearing but could see no one. The thief was gone.

In a tranquil voice she said, "Fortunately it's not too serious."

"Not serious!" Bess cried. "We lost the treasure and our wonderful vacation trip and you say it's not serious!"

Smiling, Nancy opened her handbag and displayed the missing section of the parchment map.

"I took it with me when we left the car," she explained. "As for the little ship, it's not a great loss."

"Nancy, I'm so happy I—" Bess laughed and cried, giving her friend an affectionate hug.

"There's only one thing that bothers me," Nancy said. "I can't recall the wording which was on the bottom of the *Warwick*."

"Wording?" George asked in surprise. "I didn't notice any."

"Neither did I," Bess declared. "What was it, Nancy?"

"I can remember just one word—'Little.' No doubt

it will come to me when I study the two pieces of map at home."

The girls had made only a casual inspection of the parchment, for even in a strong light the writing was difficult to make out. Nancy was eager to return home so she could look at it under a magnifying glass.

"Shall we start for River Heights?" she proposed. "We have a long drive ahead of us."

"And make no attempt to trace the person who stole the ship?" George asked in surprise.

"It wouldn't do any good. We don't have a single clue," Nancy replied. "Let's head back."

After loading the picnic hamper into the car, the three girls crowded into the front seat. Out of habit Bess reached for the button lock and pressed it down. "It does work!" she exclaimed. George frowned at her cousin but refrained from making a comment.

"On second thoughts," Nancy interposed, "I'd like to stop and talk with Ellen's father. I have a photograph to show him and he'll want to hear the good news about the map." She turned in the direction of Wayland.

Mr Smith was saddened to learn that his brother was dead. He readily identified the picture, saying, "John looked exactly like my dad at the same age."

Mr Smith expressed great pleasure over the recovery of the long-lost section of the precious map and stared at it eagerly. "This *is* my brother's torn piece," he declared positively. "Now if only I had my own half!"

"Just as soon as I get home," said Nancy, "I'll compare this with my copy of your section."

"Has Mrs Chatham actually promised to pay for the expedition?" Mrs Smith inquired. "I don't like to think of her spending so much money on something which may turn out to be a disappointment."

"Mrs Chatham wants to do it," Nancy assured her. "The trip will not only be an expedition but a holiday for her and Trixie."

Before leaving the house, the girls learned that the police had not caught the thief who had broken into the Smith home. Although Nancy did not need the stolen parchment, she feared that Spike Doty might get to the buried treasure first. That evening her father voiced a similar opinion.

"After what happened to the model of the *Warwick* you must be on your guard more than ever," he warned her, "The Browns and the others have demonstrated their ruthlessness. They will not give up, Nancy, until the fortune is theirs."

For a couple of hours she and her father studied the two sections of the map, fitting them together and trying to decipher Captain Tomlin's writing. Directions for reaching the southern Atlantic island were fairly clear, but one vital section of a word was missing.

"It would be part of the island's name," Nancy commented ruefully. "Plainly it says, 'Little —lm Island', but obviously more letters appeared on the original."

"Little Island as a clue means nothing," Carson Drew remarked, glancing up from an atlas.

"Mr Smith said the island was uncharted," Nancy reminded her father.

"That was a long time ago," Mr Drew replied. "No doubt it's on the big maps today. Anyway, I'll take another look at all the islands. Here's one. Little Palm—"

"That's it!" Nancy cried out. "Little Palm Island!"

"How do you know? How can we be sure? In this expedition a wrong guess could prove to be very costly."

"I'm not guessing, Dad. The name was carved on the bottom of the ship model which was stolen from my car today."

"Then everything seems to be cleared up," Mr Drew declared in satisfaction. "If Mrs Chatham gives her approval, we can charter a ship."

Upon learning that the lost half of the map had been recovered, Mrs Chatham was even more enthusiastic than Nancy had dared hope.

"By all means have your father engage a captain," she instructed. "And invite the Smith family and any friends you wish. We'll have a marvellous time."

Nancy telephoned Bill Tomlin, Ned, Burt Eddleton, and Dave Evans. They all instantly accepted and in a whirl of excitement Nancy began to plan her cruise wardrobe.

On Monday her hopes were suddenly deflated by her father. "I'm afraid there's not a single charter boat available now," he announced at lunch.

"Oh, Dad!" Nancy exclaimed. "Are you absolutely certain? How about a plane?"

"I've tried everywhere and everyone. No chance. I'm sorry, Nancy."

"But the Browns or Spike Doty may get to Little Palm before we do and find the buried fortune!"

That afternoon Carson Drew made several more unsuccessful attempts to find a suitable yacht. The few that were offered to him were either too large or much too small.

"Remember, dear, the thieves don't have Captain Tomlin's section of the map," Nancy's father said encouragingly.

"No," she agreed. "But don't forget that a copy of it was stolen by a member of the crew." She reminded him of the letter found in the New Kirk bank.

Days went by and Nancy chafed at the delay. She made frequent trips to Rocky Edge to discuss the situation with Mrs Chatham. Ellen had finished school for the year and come to the estate as piano teacher. Already Trixie was much better behaved.

One afternoon the child was not in sight when Nancy arrived. Ellen ran down the walk to meet the young detective, who sensed at once that something was wrong.

"Trixie has disappeared" Ellen cried. "I'm sure she has been kidnapped again!"

·15·

Detective in Disguise

HAD the kidnappers dared to abduct Trixie Chatham a second time? Nancy could not believe they would be so foolish.

"Maybe Trixie has only wandered away," she suggested.

"Oh, I hope so," Ellen said. "Mrs Chatham isn't here and I'm very worried."

"Did Trixie talk about going anywhere today?" Nancy asked.

"Why, yes, she did. She spoke of going to see you. Of course I didn't pay much attention. I told her you would be coming over but—"

"Suppose she tried to walk to River Heights? She'd definitely get lost!" Nancy exclaimed. "Come on. Hop in my car."

The two girls had expected a long search, but to their surprise they spotted Trixie a few minutes later walking along the road. Beside her was a middle-aged man in a sea captain's uniform.

"I hope that isn't Spike Doty!" Ellen exclaimed nervously.

"I think not," Nancy replied, easing on the brakes. "I can't imagine who he is."

At a closer look Trixie's companion seemed to be

quite pleasant. The child herself explained the situation and introduced the man as Captain Stryver. She had seen him walking past the estate and noticed that his uniform looked like those she had seen in pictures of men on ships. Trixie had followed him to talk about boats.

"I didn't mean to take the child away from her home," the man apologized, his weather-beaten face creasing into kindly wrinkles. "We've been gabbing a little about ships."

"He has one called the *Primrose*!" Trixie exclaimed, seizing Nancy's hand.

"I don't own her," the captain hastened to correct. "Mr Heppel, my employer, is her master."

"Is the *Primrose* for rent?" Nancy asked.

"Mr Heppel has had a lot of bad luck the past year. I'm sure he'd be glad to rent the *Primrose*. Not a prettier yacht afloat. She's tied up in New York now. I'm just here visiting my daughter."

Nancy and Ellen asked many questions, and soon were convinced that the ship was well worth an investigation. They liked Captain Stryver, and tactfully inquired if his services could be obtained for a voyage to an island in the South Atlantic.

"I know that area like a book," he said. "Nothing would suit me better than a cruise in those waters."

After talking with Captain Stryver for nearly half an hour, Nancy learned that Mr Heppel was coming to Wayland the following morning to talk to the captain. She asked to meet him.

"Come to my daughter's house at ten o'clock." He gave Nancy the address.

Since Trixie had been responsible for calling the

Primrose to their attention, neither Ellen nor Nancy felt like scolding her for wandering off. The girls brought Trixie home.

Carson Drew was pleased to learn of the *Primrose* and Captain Stryver. He went with Nancy to call on Mr Heppel the next day. The man was willing to rent his yacht for a fair sum. Pictures of it and a maritime commendation convinced the Drews of its seaworthiness.

"You'll have no problem with Captain Stryver at the wheel," said Mr Heppel. "He's honest and dependable," the owner declared, and the deal was concluded. The captain was promptly engaged and given the task of selecting a crew. Happy about the assignment, he left for New York.

Nancy's preparations for the trip were at their height later that morning when she received a telephone call from Chief McGinnis of the River Heights police force.

"We have a lead, Nancy," he said. The chief was a long-time friend of the Drews. "Spike Doty's address." He rattled off the number and name of the street. "It's a boarding-house."

"That's in the worst district of town," Nancy commented.

"A couple of our men are down there now," the chief said. "Dressed like town hoods. They're waiting for Doty to appear."

"Are you sure he still lives in that apartment house?" Nancy asked.

"The landlady verified it but said he hasn't been to his room since the night before last."

"I'd like to take a look around myself."

"If you want a police escort—"

"Oh, no. I don't want to scare Doty off or be too conspicuous. As a matter of fact—" She stopped speaking. "I'll be okay. Thanks just the same."

Not wishing to reveal over the phone a plan she had suddenly thought of, Nancy assured him she would take no chances and said goodbye. She went to her room and from the rear of her closet pulled out a dark-coloured dress that was out of style, a pair of old brown shoes, and a bottle of grey dusting powder for the hair.

"I hope this'll work." she said to herself. "Too bad Hannah and Dad aren't here so I could tell them my plan."

Quickly she changed clothes and brushed some of the powder into her hair, giving it a grey tinge. She combed it to give a straggly appearance. Fully disguised, Nancy posed in front of the full-length mirror in the hall.

"Well, Mrs Frisby, are you ready to do some house cleanin'?" Nancy asked her reflection. Could she trap the thief in this disguise? A broad grin spread across her face as she answered, "Give me a broom and I'll sweep Doty into jail!"

In a short while Nancy was on her way. She parked her car in a pleasant neighbourhood several blocks from Doty's boarding-house. Then, hunching her shoulders and lowering her head, she walked the rest of the distance. An untidy landlady answered her knock.

"What do you want?" she bellowed, glaring at the old woman before her.

A crude letter holder hung on the wall. Chalked on it were several names and room numbers. Doty's was 22.

Could she trap the thief in this disguise?
Nancy wondered

"I come t' clean up Mr Doty's room," Nancy announced. "Kin I start right now? Just tell me where you keep everything and open his door, please. I'll be in and out in a jiffy."

The red-haired woman looked surprised but led Nancy up the sagging stairway. "All the cleaning stuff's in the cupboard down the hall. His room's over there. Door's always unlocked. I can't figure that guy. He's been out for almost two days and wants his room cleaned. For who? The mice?"

Without waiting for an answer, the landlady started downstairs, leaving Nancy alone. The young sleuth opened the door to Spike Doty's room. It was shabby and contained only a desk, a bed, and a chair, all piled with old newspapers and torn envelopes. She pretended to straighten up the room, hunting through the papers for a clue to any accomplices of Doty's or to his whereabouts if he had left town.

"What if he has gone to Little Palm Island!" Nancy frowned at the possibility.

As she continued to "clean up," a car stopped in front of the apartment house, but she was unaware of this. Fred and Irene Brown, somewhat disguised, alighted. They presented themselves at the door and inquired about Spike Doty.

"For someone who's not around he sure gets enough visitors," the landlady said irritably.

"Who else came here?" Fred Brown asked quickly.

"The cleaning woman for one. Look, I'm getting tired answering questions. Doty's not here. That's all I know."

"We do hate to take up your time, but could we talk somewhere in private?" Mrs Brown inquired with exaggerated politeness. "We're Mr and Mrs Fred Brown."

As she spoke, a young man brushed past them and started upstairs.

"Wait a minute, fella. You don't live here," the landlady shouted after him.

"I'm visiting a friend," he called back, without turning round.

The landlady threw up her hands in disgust and shook her head, then turned to the couple. "In here," she said and led them into a small living-room.

The Browns asked a few more questions. "This cleaning woman you mentioned, do you know how we can get in touch with her?" the man asked.

"You won't have to go far. She's still upstairs."

At that moment Nancy was about ready to give up what was proving to be a fruitless search.

"A wasted afternoon!" she admonished herself. "I'd better do a little cleaning before the landlady comes barging in. Or before Doty returns!"

She had just folded the last newspaper when the knob began turning and the door creaked open.

A Hoax

"NED! What are you doing here?" Nancy cried in astonishment.

"I spotted you when you parked your car. In that get-up I knew you were up to something and decided to find out what it was," Ned answered quickly. "But I didn't want to interrupt your sleuthing so I stayed behind a distance. Listen, Fred and Irene Brown are downstairs," he added as a knock came at the door.

"Hey, what's going on?" the landlady asked, stepping inside. "I thought you said you were visiting a friend." She glared at Ned, who did not answer.

The woman turned to Nancy. "There's a man and his wife downstairs who want to see you—I don't know what about!"

Nancy squeezed Ned's hand, signalling him to watch her. Without saying a word to each other, they followed the landlady downstairs.

As she turned into the living-room, Nancy and Ned quickly side-stepped her, dashed outside and got into his car. As they shot away from the kerb, Nancy turned to look back. The landlady, anger in her eyes, was flailing her arms wildly at Mr and Mrs Brown and shooing them down the front steps.

"Guess she didn't like them either," Nancy thought.

Ned drove Nancy to the spot where she had parked the convertible, then waved goodbye, saying he would see her later.

Nancy went directly home, and after removing her disguise, glanced through the mail which had been delivered earlier. There was a letter from her Aunt Eloise but most of the envelopes contained advertisements. One, however, was addressed to her in pencil and had been posted the day before. The message inside had been scrawled on a sheet of cheap notepaper. It read:

> Dear Miss Drew. I tuk yer boat
> cos I need money but I can't sell it.
> You can hav it back for a few bucks.
> It says somethin important inside.
> Don't tell the cops and come alone
> on foot to 47 White Strete.

Nancy read the message a second time, then ran to the kitchen to show it to Hannah.

"This practically shatters one of my best theories!" she declared. "I had a hunch that the model ship had been stolen by Fred and Irene Brown. This note seems to prove I was wrong."

"It appears to have been written by a young or poorly educated person," the housekeeper commented as she looked at the misspelled words. "He signs himself Ted." After a pause Hannah asked, "What will you do, Nancy?"

"I don't know. Strange I didn't notice anything carved inside the *Warwick* model." She paused a moment. "It's a long distance to White Street, but this note says to come on foot—"

"Nancy, I can't permit you to walk through that area!" Hannah Gruen exclaimed.

"I'll take the car," Nancy said. "And maybe I won't have to go inside the house."

Mrs Gruen did not approve of the mission and begged Nancy to be careful. The young detective was well on her way to White Street when it occurred to her it was odd that Ted knew her name and address.

She had no intention of walking into a trap and made up her mind she would not enter the house. Instead, she would insist that the model ship be brought to her.

As Nancy pulled up before number 47, a shabby, old-fashioned house, she saw a boy with a sharp, taut face seated on the porch. Evidently he had been expecting her, because he quickly came to the car.

"Are you Ted?" she asked, trying not to seem unfriendly.

"That's me," he answered gruffly, "but you was supposed to come on foot. You want the boat?"

"Yes I do, Ted. May I ask why you stole it from my car?"

"You kin ask all you want but I ain't givin' no answers," the boy retorted saucily. "The boat's upstairs."

"You must bring it to me."

"Grandma won't let it go without the money," the boy said stubbornly. "She's sick in bed and we need the cash. If you want to see the ship, you gotta come upstairs."

Nancy was in a quandary. A chance to obtain the needed information on the exact location of the treasure might be lost! Reluctantly she climbed up a flight of worn stairs through a dark hall to a wood-panelled bedroom.

"Grandma, this is the girl," Ted said by way of introduction.

He disappeared, closing the door behind him. Nancy was startled by his sudden departure but tried not to show alarm. She attempted to reassure herself that nothing was amiss. The *Warwick* was in plain sight on the table beside the bed.

"How much money you got on you?" the elderly woman asked in a squeaky voice, her face half hidden under the covers.

Nancy opened her purse and pulled out several bills.

A gleam of satisfaction lit up the old lady's eyes as she reached for the money. "The ship's yours. Only promise you won't make trouble for Ted."

"Very well," Nancy consented, and turned from the bed to lift the model from the table.

Instantly the elderly woman threw off the covers and leaped from the bed. Irene Brown!

Simultaneously, Fred Brown appeared from inside a cupboard and tried to pin Nancy's arms behind her. As she struggled violently, the ship crashed to the floor.

Although Nancy fought with all her strength, she was no match for her assailants. In a moment they held her fast.

"The clever Miss Drew wasn't so smart this time!" the man gloated, taking a handkerchief from his pocket to gag her.

Securely bound, Nancy was shoved through a cupboard with a concealed door which connected with an adjoining vacant house. She was seated at a table and told to write a letter to Hannah Gruen. Nancy was to request that the piece of map found in the model ship be sent to her at once.

"Don't try to get away with anything in this letter," Fred Brown threatened.

In despair, Nancy slowly composed the message. She knew she could not include anything that would indicate her true predicament. There was just one faint hope of outwitting the sinister couple. Accordingly she wrote:

> *Please give bearer the copy of the*
> *map found in the model ship.*
> *Nancy*

"Perhaps if I concentrate very hard, I can get a thought wave to Hannah, so she'll make a copy—but not an exact one," Nancy told herself. "It's my one hope."

Unknown to Nancy, Mr Drew and Ned already were alarmed over her long absence from home. Informed by the worried housekeeper that Nancy had gone to the White Street address, they set off in Ned's car to search for her.

"It isn't like Nancy to stay away so long without any explanation," the lawyer declared as Ned parked at the kerb. "She may have walked into a trap."

As they rang the doorbell again and again Ned remarked that Nancy's car was not in sight. He knocked on the door several times but received no response.

At last Mr Drew became impatient. Trying the door and finding it unlocked, he entered with Ned close behind.

"Why, this place is deserted," he observed as they

looked into the empty ground-floor rooms. "We do have the correct address, I hope."

"This is it all right. How about upstairs?" Ned asked, leading the way this time.

The first door confronting them opened into the bedroom where Nancy had been taken prisoner. Before them was an overturned chair and lying beside it the broken model of the *Warwick*!

"There has been a struggle!" Mr Drew exclaimed, losing his usual calm. "Something has happened to Nancy!"

With increasing alarm he and Ned searched the entire house but found no trace of the missing girl. While Mr Drew continued to look for clues in the room where the struggle had taken place, Ned went to question the neighbours. He returned with a discouraging report.

"I couldn't contact anyone, Mr Drew. Must have rung four or five doorbells, too. The place next to this one is vacant."

"To the east or on the west side?" the lawyer asked.

"The east. It adjoins this room."

Mr Drew had been fingering a small object which he now showed the young man. It was an ornamental brooch.

"I picked this up from the floor of the closet," the lawyer explained. "I have a hunch it came from Nancy's dress and she dropped it as a clue. Ned, suppose you call Hannah Gruen and ask her if Nancy was wearing the brooch when she left."

"I'll be back in a minute," Ned said, starting away. "Maybe Nancy has arrived home since we left."

Carson Drew was not so optimistic as he returned

to his investigation of the closet. He found something which previously had escaped his attention. Although skilfully disguised with wallpaper, the back of the closet was made of wood instead of plaster. When he tapped his knuckles against it, there was a hollow sound.

"It's a door!" he exclaimed. "The pattern of the paper hides the outline!"

Mr Drew pushed hard on the panel but could not budge it. Again and again he tried but to no avail.

He was mulling over the problem when Ned returned and reported, "The brooch was on Nancy's dress. And she hasn't come home."

"There's no question about it, Ned. Nancy has been captured. I'm positive she was taken through this sliding panel to the next house."

"What!" Ned exclaimed.

"The panel has been locked on the other side. I've tried to get it open but—"

"Let's break it down," the young man urged.

"And tip off the kidnappers? No, I think we'd better proceed quietly," Mr Drew answered. Just then he spied a small keyhole. "This is an ordinary lock," he said.

From his pocket he took a bunch of keys. One by one he tried them. The next to the last unlocked the door.

Never dreaming that her father and Ned were so close, Nancy remained alone in a tiny second-floor storeroom, ventilated by only one small window. She sat on an old wooden chair, gagged and tied so tightly her bones ached.

"If only something good would happen!" she thought unhappily. "What will Hannah do when she gets my note?"

At that very moment Irene Brown was ringing the doorbell of the Drew home. Behind the hedge her husband watched, pleased with himself. No one but the housekeeper was at home, he knew, and should she become suspicious, she could not call for help. He had just cut the telephone wires.

His wife greeted Mrs Gruen pleasantly and said, "I have a note here for you from Miss Drew. I don't know what it says, but she asked me to wait for an answer."

"Will you come inside?" Hannah asked.

· 17 ·

Puzzling Paper

AFTER thoroughly searching the vacant house, Carson Drew and Ned were ready to give up. They had found no trace of Nancy.

"I was so sure she was here," the lawyer declared. He and Ned had reached the attic floor, which was dark and suffocatingly stuffy. "But maybe she was taken to another hideout."

"Listen!" Ned said.

They could hear a distinct scratching noise, as if someone were clawing against a plaster wall. Tracing the sound, Mr Drew saw a door in a dingy corner of the room.

"Maybe she's in there!" he exclaimed, pulling at the knob.

Nancy, bound and gagged, stared in disbelief. Ned tore off the handkerchief while Mr Drew untied her bonds.

"Are you okay?" he asked apprehensively. "You look pale."

"I'm all right," she assured him and her father, "but I'm afraid we've run into a real calamity."

"What do you mean?" Mr Drew asked.

"The Browns made me write a note to Hannah ordering her to deliver Captain Tomlin's map to them."

"How long ago was that, Nancy?" her father inquired quickly.

"At least half an hour."

"Perhaps we can catch them!" Carson Drew exclaimed.

Leaving Ned to look for Nancy's car, he and his daughter drove home at top speed. Entering the house, they discovered Hannah Gruen down on her knees examining the telephone.

"Nancy, you're safe!" she exclaimed joyfully. "Oh, I'm so relieved."

"Did someone come here with a note from me?" Nancy asked anxiously.

"Yes, a woman. She left about ten minutes ago."

"That was Irene Brown!"

"I guessed as much, so I tried to call the police, but the telephone wires had been cut."

"You gave her the map?" Nancy asked.

"That was what you requested me to do," the housekeeper responded.

"Yes, I did. Oh, I can't blame you. You had no way of knowing that I didn't want you to carry out the instructions."

"All the same, I guessed it from the wording in your note," the housekeeper declared, ending the suspense. "I gave Mrs Brown a map, but it will never do her and her husband any good. And it serves them right."

"Oh, Hannah, you're wonderful!" Nancy laughed happily and hugged her. "How did you manage to outwit her?"

"It was very easy. I knew you kept both sections of the map in your desk—Captain Tomlin's original and the copy of Mr Smith's portion. I found an old piece of parchment in the desk and tore it diagonally. Then I quickly traced the original, leaving out many details and making several changes!"

"Mrs Brown never once suspected?" Nancy asked, chuckling.

"No, she must have thought what I gave her was genuine, because she thanked me sweetly and went away."

"Hannah, you're as clever as any detective of my acquaintance," Mr Drew said with a grin.

"I'm really grateful," Nancy added.

"There's just one thing that troubles me," Hannah said. "I copied the name of the island on the paper."

"Let's not worry about that," said Mr Drew, "since you left out some of the directions."

While the housekeeper was preparing a late dinner, Mr Drew went to a neighbour's and called the telephone company to report the cut wires. A repair man was sent at once and within a short time the Drews' phone was back in service.

As they finished dinner the telephone rang and Nancy rose to answer it. She recognized Ned's voice.

"Hello, Nancy," he said, talking hurriedly. "I found your car. I'll bring it over as soon as I can. Right now I'm at the police station, and Chief McGinnis wants you to come at once."

"Now?"

"Yes. Fred and Irene Brown have been taken into custody. The chief wants an identification."

"Be there in a minute. 'Bye."

Nancy and her father went immediately to the police station. To their delight they learned that Ned had led the police to 47 White Street and aided them in nabbing the Browns when the couple had returned to release Nancy.

"May we talk with them?" she asked the police chief.

"Go ahead and good luck. We haven't been able to get a word out of either of them."

Mr Drew and Nancy talked with the couple. They learned nothing from Fred, who denied the kidnapping of Nancy from Emerson.

"Forget it," he said. "It's the word of two against one."

Irene Brown proved to be less discreet. Nancy played upon the woman's feelings by intimating that Spike Doty was in jail and had made damaging revelations which implicated the couple.

"Why, the double-crosser!" Mrs Brown cried furiously. "He was the one who first learned about the fortune, and now he tries to throw all the blame on us!"

"Then you've been working with him?" Carson Drew asked quietly.

"Not any more."

"Rorke, perhaps?" Nancy inquired, watching the woman's face intently.

"Never heard of him," Irene Brown answered, but her eyes wavered—indicating to her questioners that she was not telling the truth.

"What did you do with the map you obtained from our housekeeper?" Carson Drew demanded. He had learned from the police that the paper had not been found in the Browns' possession.

"We sold it," Irene answered briefly.

"To Rorke?" the lawyer asked.

"Look, I don't have to tell you anything."

Realizing she had talked too much, Irene Brown fell into a sullen silence and refused to answer any more questions. Before leaving headquarters, Nancy and Mr Drew again talked with Chief McGinnis.

"I'll have the Browns held without bail," the chief said. "Kidnapping is a serious charge."

Although the man and his wife were behind bars, Nancy remained uneasy. Spike Doty and the mysterious Mr Rorke were free and both were determined to get the Tomlin treasure.

"Have they learned the location of Little Palm Island?" Nancy wondered. "Are they on their way to it?"

She phoned Mrs Chatham, who was as impatient as Nancy to get the treasure hunt under way. The widow telephoned Captain Stryver, urging him to speed preparations so that the *Primrose* could sail from New York as soon as possible.

"I can have her ready by tomorrow," he said. "If I had a little more time, though, I could be more selective about the crew."

"We can't afford to waste another day," the woman told him.

The next morning Carson Drew, the Marvins, and the Faynes said goodbye to their daughters at the airport.

"Wish I were going along," the lawyer said. "Have a good time and bring home the treasure!"

"At least I'll get a good tan." Nancy laughed, squeezing her father's hand and kissing him.

The travelling group consisted of Mrs Chatham

Trixie, the three Smiths, Bill Tomlin, and Nancy's special friends.

Bess's boyfriend, Dave Evans, was a blond, rangy, green-eyed boy who was on the Emerson football team. Burt Eddleton, George's friend, was also blond, but shorter and husky. He, too, played on the team.

With a grin Burt said, "A treasure hunt on a lonely island should have at least one pirate. I'm applying for the job."

Dave called, "I'll give you a patch for one eye!" The others laughed.

The trip to New York was fast. Taxis were hailed and the group headed for the dock and their first glimpse of the *Primrose*.

"Isn't she beautiful!" Bess exclaimed, gazing at the trim yacht.

As Nancy looked at the ship, her attention was diverted by a small piece of paper which had just blown from behind a crate on the dock. Wondering if it had been dropped by someone aboard the *Primrose*, she went over to pick it up. The next instant she stared in astonishment. A hand-printed message on the sheet read:

MEET YOU ON THE DOCK WEDNESDAY MIDNIGHT.
                                                    SPIKE

"That was last night!" Nancy thought.

Her friends, with the exception of Ned, were already going aboard and being greeted by Captain Stryver.

"Find something?" Ned asked Nancy.

She showed him the paper. "Wow!" he exclaimed. "I wonder who received this."

"Ned, I think we should tell the captain that Spike

might have placed a bomb aboard or tampered with the machinery."

The two reported the incident at once and a thorough search was made. Nothing was found.

Although Nancy was relieved, she had an uneasy feeling that something was amiss. She would certainly keep her eyes open.

The *Primrose* was a comfortable, seaworthy craft which ploughed through deep waves with scarcely a roll. Even so, Mrs Chatham, a poor sailor, soon was confined to her cabin with a mild case of seasickness. Ellen and Trixie shared an adjoining stateroom.

Left mostly to themselves, Nancy, Ned, and the other couples thoroughly enjoyed the daylight hours on deck. The second night out they danced to records and held an impromptu entertainment. Bill Tomlin, a talented guitar player, was asked to accompany Ellen. The young people would not let her stop until she had sung several selections. All applauded her loudly. Finally she begged off, saying she must put Trixie to bed.

"Come back soon," Nancy urged.

Trixie began to pout. "Ellen's my room-mate. I want her to stay with me!"

Ellen merely smiled and promised a bedtime story, which Nancy was sure would put the child to sleep. A few minutes later Bill Tomlin slipped away from the group and followed Ellen down portside. Presently their voices, talking and laughing, could be heard against the sound of splashing waves.

The other couples strolled about the deck, enjoying the mild breezes and stopping to watch the moon's reflection ripple on the water.

"Nancy," said Ned, "since there's no trouble on the *Primrose*, I hope you'll forget about mysteries or treasure until we get to the island."

"It'll be won—"

"Help! He-e-e-lp!" a girl's cry interrupted Nancy's answer.

"That sounds like Bess!" Nancy exclaimed.

"It is!" Ned said. He pointed to a figure just surfacing in the water.

Treachery

In a flash Dave had jumped in after Bess. Ned rushed to a deck telephone to ask that the *Primrose* be stopped.

As the young people watched Bess and Dave swim towards the yacht, Captain Stryver and Mrs Chatham came on deck.

"What's all the commotion about?" she asked.

"Bess went overboard," Nancy replied. "We don't know why."

In a few minutes the two swimmers reached the side of the *Primrose*. A rope ladder had been thrown down. Bess, shivering and her dress and hair limp, climbed up slowly. Dave followed.

Their friends plied them with questions. "Did you fall in?" "Were you pushed overboard?"

Bess's teeth chattered as she gratefully accepted a large beach towel from George and wrapped it snugly about her. Instead of answering immediately, big tears began to roll down her cheeks.

"Sit here," Nancy said, indicating a deck chair. "You've had a shock. Take your time and tell us what happened."

Bess said haltingly, "I asked Dave to get my sweater from the other side of the yacht. While he was gone, I rested my arms on the rail over there and suddenly it gave way. I screamed so you wouldn't leave me behind."

As Bess finished her explanation, Bill Tomlin arrived on the scene. He went to examine the rail. Finally he said, "This is part of a gate which wasn't latched properly."

George turned to Nancy, "Do you think it was a case of sabotage?"

Nancy frowned. "I can't get Spike out of my mind. He may have tampered with that latch before we came aboard."

The next day Nancy came on deck to find a tough-looking young sailor at the wheel of the *Primrose*. She did not like his appearance and recalled that Captain Stryver had been compelled to hire any available men.

"Good morning," she greeted him pleasantly. "I'm Nancy Drew. Your name?"

"Snorky."

"Snorky, have you seen Captain Stryver?"

"He's sick in his cabin," the man answered, a suggestion of satisfaction in his voice. He spun the wheel, bringing the yacht around slightly. "The mate's flat on his back, too," he added.

"How strange both of them are ill!" Nancy said to herself.

She walked aft. Meeting Ned, she mentioned the illness of the two officers.

"There's another mystery, too," he said soberly. "We seem to have changed direction. I think I'll talk with Bill Tomlin. He's been charting our course since we left New York."

He was gone about fifteen minutes. When he rejoined Nancy, Bill was with him.

"I was right," Ned announced grimly. "Bill thinks

we're off course. He has piloted motor-boats all his life and studied navigation."

"I want to ask that guy Snorky a few questions," Bill said, and the three went forward.

Upon being questioned, the crewman took the attitude that guiding the *Primrose* was his responsibility, and not that of anyone else.

"We may be a little off course," he admitted, "but don't worry about it."

"Swing her back now," Bill Tomlin ordered sharply, "or we'll talk to the captain."

Angrily Snorky brought the bow of the ship around so the *Primrose* once more was heading south. No sooner had the trio moved away, however, than the sailor again altered the direction. Bill Tomlin, who felt the lurch of the vessel as it turned, became irritated.

"Please don't get into a fight with Snorky," Nancy pleaded. "Let's talk to Captain Stryver."

At once the young people went to his quarters. Barely able to sit up in bed, the officer listened in alarm to their story. He declared he would be top-side in a few hours.

"I don't think we should leave Snorky in charge," said Bill. "He's taking us directly eastward."

"East!" the captain exclaimed. "I've got to get out of this bed!"

"No, you mustn't exert yourself when you're so weak," Nancy protested. "If Bill may have the chart, I'm sure he can check on our course."

"The chart's in my desk," the captain mumbled, sinking back on the pillow.

Bill found it and in a few seconds cried, "We're way off course!"

"I think Snorky is deliberately trying to delay us," Ned stated. "But no one else can be spared to take his place."

"I can steer the *Primrose*," Bill declared confidently. "There's nothing to it. Come on. We'll take care of Snorky!"

He and Ned went forward. There was a brief argument with the sailor. When he refused to give up the wheel, the boys bodily removed him and Bill took over.

The remainder of the day went along quietly, except that Snorky glowered angrily as he washed down the decks. All this time Nancy kept thinking of the note she had found. Was Snorky a friend of Spike's? And had Spike arranged with Snorky to take the yacht on a wrong course?

Another thought came to her. She confided it to Bess and George. "Do you suppose he's responsible for the captain's illness? Maybe he bribed the cook to put something in his food."

The next morning Bill Tomlin was taken ill while at the wheel of the *Primrose*. His attack was a mild one, though, and he refused to leave his post.

Unknown to the others, Nancy and George kept an eye on the galley. They became well acquainted with the cook, winning the man's gratitude by peeling a large pan of potatoes. After they had talked with him for half an hour, the girls decided he had not connived with Snorky.

Nancy whispered to George, "Possibly Snorky engaged the cook in conversation and waited for the chance to contaminate the food when he wasn't looking." George agreed.

Next, Nancy asked Ned to slip into the forecastle and hunt for a clue among Snorky's belongings. His possessions did not reveal anything suspicious. Ned ran his hand under the mattress of the sailor's bunk.

"Here's something!" he thought, holding up a small envelope.

It contained an odourless white powder. Ned felt certain that Snorky had used some of it to taint the ship's food. He reported his find to Nancy.

"I have an idea!" she said. "Wait here for me."

Nancy ran to the galley and grabbed a large salt shaker. She took a small polythene bag from a drawer then hurried back.

"Ned, substitute this salt for the powder!" she said. "Put the white powder in this plastic bag. We'll keep it for evidence."

Taking her friends into her confidence, Nancy organized a watch over the galley. On the pretext of helping the overburdened cook, the girls even assisted in serving the meals. At lunch Ned complained his food tasted very salty.

"Snorky is sly," Nancy observed to George as they discussed the situation. "We'll have to tighten our watch. If we don't, I'm afraid something dreadful may happen before we reach Little Palm."

An unexpected change in the weather temporarily drove all thought of Snorky from everyone's mind. The barometer fell steadily and within a few hours waves were breaking over the decks.

Although weakened by his illness, Captain Stryver resumed command of the ship, relieving the weary

Bill Tomlin. As the day wore on, the gale became worse so that everyone was driven below. Even the cook went to his bunk.

Nancy, however, grew restless. Deciding that Snorky should be watched, she went to look for him. The sailor could not be found, even after Ned and Bill had joined the search.

"Say, maybe he was washed overboard!" Bill said uneasily. "I'll ask the captain if he has seen him."

Nancy did not agree. Without telling anyone where she was going, the young detective went below to the galley. Before she reached it, the door opened and the missing sailor came out, carrying a box in his arms. He turned in the opposite direction without seeing Nancy.

"Now what was he doing in there?" she thought. "He must have had more poison powder for the food, and he's carrying away the good stuff for himself?"

Thoroughly alarmed, she started up the ladder, intending to warn her friends not to eat anything served. Nancy was midway up the rungs when the yacht gave a lurch.

She was thrown off balance. Unable to steady herself, Nancy toppled backwards, falling to the deck. Her head struck hard and everything went black before her eyes. When she opened them, she was lying on a couch in Captain Stryver's cabin. Her anxious friends were grouped about her.

"You okay?" Ned asked, pressing a cup of water to her lips.

Nancy sat up, trying to recall what had happened. Her eyes roved from one face to another.

"What is it, Nancy?" Ned asked, sensing that something was wrong.

"Don't eat," she whispered. "Whatever you do, don't touch anything coming from the galley!"

Nancy told how she had seen Snorky stealing away from the ship's galley.

"He's trying to keep us from reaching Little Palm Island," she ended her story wearily. "Will you help me to my cabin?"

While Bess and George made Nancy comfortable in her bunk, Bill Tomlin and Ned sought the captain. The three of them searched the ship. They found Snorky hiding in the hold, presumably to avoid Stryver. The captain demanded a reason for his conduct.

"I wasn't within a mile of the galley," the man whined. "I was hunting in the hold for some extra clothes of mine."

Suspicious, Captain Stryver ordered another sailor to send the cook up with a sample of every dish of food which was to be served at dinner. Commanded to eat, Snorky sullenly obeyed, refusing only to taste a bowl of split pea soup.

"What do you know about this?" Stryver asked the cook.

"Nothing, sir. Snorky must have sneaked into the galley when I was in the dining-room."

"Throw the soup overboard," the captain instructed the cook. "As for Snorky, we'll lock him up until we reach port."

A thorough search was made of his cabin. No evidence against him was found other than more of the white powder. Nancy had hoped a clue connecting him with Spike would turn up. None had, but she did not swerve from her original theory that Snorky was working with people interested in the treasure.

To everyone's relief, the remainder of the trip was uneventful. Late one afternoon the *Primrose* came within sight of Little Palm Island. Through binoculars it looked like a tiny crescent-shaped spot of green, its sandy shores lined solidly with gently waving palms.

The ship nosed her way cautiously ahead and at length dropped anchor a safe distance from the pounding surf. Captain Stryver, Bill Tomlin, and Ned decided to row ashore to make a preliminary investigation.

Anxiously those aboard the *Primrose* watched the little craft row away. A few minutes later a crewman came up hurriedly to the group to report that Snorky had escaped from the cabin where he had been locked up.

"He's nowhere on the ship!" the seaman added. "He must have jumped overboard and swum to shore."

"How frightful!" exclaimed Mrs Chatham. "Now none of us will be safe!"

Nancy's uneasiness for the men in the rowing-boat increased. Captain Stryver's party might be attacked!

·19·

Impostor

To the relief of everyone aboard the *Primrose*, the small boat returned from the island in less than an hour.

"What's the report?" Nancy asked eagerly as Captain Stryver climbed aboard the *Primrose*, followed by Ned and Bill.

"This side of the island seems to be deserted," the captain replied. "We did find considerable evidence of digging, though."

"Oh dear!" Nancy exclaimed. "That means someone has reached the spot ahead of us! And Snorky has escaped!"

"What!" Stryver shouted, and went off to get more details.

Nancy said to Ned, "Snorky has probably joined Spike and maybe others on the island."

A few minutes later Captain Stryver came top-side and said all the men except Mr Smith would go back to the island in search of the fugitive.

"When it's safe for you girls to land, I'll let you know."

Mrs Chatham, Mrs Smith, Nancy, and the other girls remained on deck. Anxiously they watched the men go ashore, then vanish behind a fringe of palms.

Mrs Chatham walked the deck nervously. "Oh, I wish they'd return!" she said over and over.

"Listen!" Nancy cried suddenly. "I thought I heard someone shout!"

"So did I!" agreed Ellen, who was standing beside her.

A moment later the watchers saw several men on the beach. Seizing the binoculars, Nancy adjusted them to her eyes.

"They've caught Snorky!" she exclaimed. "Another man, too. I think he's Spike Doty."

"Who's that in the white suit?" Mrs Chatham asked. She had observed him join the group on the beach.

Nancy replied, "His big hat is pulled too low for me to get a good look at him."

As she watched intently Nancy could tell that the newcomer was arguing with Captain Stryver. He seemed to be ordering the *Primrose* party away from the island. This was substantiated by Ned and a sailor when they rowed back to the yacht a few minutes later.

"That Heyborn fellow in white claims he owns the island," Ned explained. "He won't permit us to land or to dig."

"But there's been a lot of digging on the island already," Nancy said in quick protest.

"He claims he knew nothing about it. We've caught Snorky, and that other guy in the blue jeans may be the one who robbed the Smith home," Ned declared. "I came back to get Nancy and Ellen for a positive identification."

The two girls set off for the island with Ned. Heyborn had disappeared before their arrival. One glance satisfied them that Snorky's companion was indeed Spike Doty.

Captain Stryver said, "Mr Heyborn, the owner of the island, volunteered to look after the prisoners, but I declined the offer. I don't entirely trust him."

He lowered his voice when he saw the man in the white suit returning. Darkness was coming on, and although Nancy tried her best, she could not obtain a good view of the bearded man's face buried under the low-brimmed hat.

"Please let us search," Ellen pleaded. "It means so much to Mrs Chatham and my family."

"Sorry, I can't allow that," he said irritably.

Ned and Ellen would have pressed the matter further but Nancy gave them a warning glance.

"I can see your point of view," she said to the owner. "We'll leave at once."

Her friends stared, aghast. A few minutes later, on their way to the yacht, they demanded an explanation.

"I wanted to throw him off the track," Nancy told them. "I don't believe he's the owner of Little Palm Island. He must be a pal of Snorky and Spike."

Ellen was thoroughly alarmed. "We just do something to stop him then. But what?"

"I have a little plan," Nancy said.

She proposed that a few of them wait until after dark, then steal back to the island and investigate.

"Where does Mr Heyborn live?" she asked Ned. "He must have some kind of house in the woods."

"It's a cabin," Ned replied. "We saw it from a distance while we were chasing Spike and Snorky among the trees."

"Then we should begin there," Nancy stated. "Maybe Bill will go with us."

Ellen, who was somewhat timid, did not care to be

included in the adventure. Bill Tomlin, however, was enthusiastic.

"Nothing would suit me better than to round up that gang," he said.

In a short while the trio quietly launched a boat. With muffled oars they rowed to the beach as thick clouds scudded overhead, obscuring the moon.

"No sign of anyone around," Ned whispered as the boat grated on the beach. "All the same, we'd better be on our guard."

After camouflaging their craft with palm leaves, the three moved stealthily through the tropical woods. Presently they came to a worn path which led them to a one-storey building made of palmetto logs.

"That's the place," Ned told his companions. "Now what?"

"Somehow we must look inside," Nancy whispered to the boys. "I suspect that the real owner of the island may have been taken prisoner by the man who claims to be Heyborn. And I'll bet that the impostor is here, too."

Moving to the rear of the cabin, flashlights off, the three paused beside a window. Nancy pressed her face against the screen.

"Let me have your flashlight, Ned," she whispered. "I think a woman is lying on the bed, bound and gagged."

"Maybe it's Mrs Heyborn," he replied.

Nancy flashed the beam, drawing in her breath at what she saw. A sleeping woman lay on the bed, her ankles tied together and chained to one of the posts!

Horrified, Nancy raised the screen and called to her softly. At first the figure did not stir. When the woman

The sleeping woman was chained to a bedpost

did lift her head from the pillow, she shivered in fear.

"Don't be afraid!" Nancy called in a soothing voice. "We're here to help you."

"Please! Please!" the woman pleaded pitifully. "My husband and son are prisoners, too!"

Ned hoisted Nancy through the window so that she could talk with less fear of discovery. He and Bill waited outside, keeping watch.

"Are you Mrs Heyborn?" Nancy asked, and introduced herself.

"Yes," the woman murmured. "Two men landed here a few days ago in a boat. They accepted our hospitality, then made us prisoners. My husband and son are chained in another room. Oh, I hope they're all right!"

"What became of the boat? We didn't see it when we landed."

"Gone," Mrs Heyborn revealed. "I heard one of the men—the others call him Spike—say it would return in a day or two with a lot more digging equipment."

After examining the woman's bonds, Nancy realized she could not hope to release her without the key to the padlock.

"I'll be back," she said in a comforting tone. "Then I'll get this lock off."

Tiptoeing to the window, she climbed out and rejoined Bill and Ned. She told them everything she had learned.

"We must capture the man who is impersonating Mr Heyborn and get the key to the padlock from him right away. And, boys, the real Mr Heyborn and his son are prisoners somewhere."

At the rear of the building was a screened porch which the young people had barely noticed. As they walked around the house they saw that a bunk had been set up in the enclosure. A man was stretched out on it.

"That must be the impostor!" Nancy whispered to her companions. "If we're quiet, we can take him without a struggle!"

Making no sound, the three opened the door of the porch and slipped inside. Ned took a rope from his pocket and bound the man's feet. The startled prisoner, awakening, struggled to a sitting position. A false beard lay on a nearby chair with a big straw hat and a white coat.

"Mr Rorke!" Nancy exclaimed.

He tried to break free, but Ned and Bill held him securely while Nancy tied his hands behind his back. The boys searched his pockets and turned the man's keys over to Nancy. She hurried to Mrs Heyborn, freeing her, then her husband and young son.

The little boy grinned sleepily. "This is just like in a story book," he remarked.

When Mr Heyborn heard the entire story, he was amazed. He assured the young people that he would not interfere with the Tomlin treasure hunt.

"Dig to your hearts' content," he urged them generously. "My wife and I came here to enjoy a peaceful existence. And our son loves it. I'm a naturalist, connected with the American Museum, and have been studying the flora of the island. All I ask is the privilege of continuing my work without interruption."

With Spike Doty, Snorky, and Rorke captured, Nancy believed there would be no further trouble. A ship-to-shore telephone call was made to government officials, requesting that a boat be dispatched from the nearest point to take charge of the three prisoners.

On the way back to the yacht Nancy questioned Rorke. He admitted learning of the treasure from the son of the first mate of the *Warwick*, not the *Sea Hawk*. The man, now dead, was not named Gambrell. The mate had stolen Captain John Tomlin's copy of the half section of the parchment map, but had lost it. The only words he could remember on the paper, he had told his son, were "Pa" and "South Atlantic."

Rorke had discovered the whereabouts of the captain's twin brother, now known as Tomlin Smith. Accordingly, Rorke offered Ellen's father money for his section of the map.

At that point in the confession, the rowing-boat reached the *Primrose*. Nancy decided to wait until morning for the remainder of the account. Dawn was coming up and the adventurers needed rest.

Nancy fell into a deep sleep, but early in the morning she awakened with a start. From somewhere a young man's voice was callling, "Nancy Drew! Come out on deck! It's important!"

She quickly put on a robe and tiptoed to the door. No one was in the corridor.

"Did I dream I was being called?" Nancy wondered.

The summons was not repeated. Nancy went back to bed, but not to sleep. She had just begun to feel drowsy when she heard the summons again. This time the sounds seemed to come through the open porthole.

Once more Nancy got up, poked her head out, and looked to the deck above. The young sailor who had announced the disappearance of Snorky was leaning over the rail. He smiled down at her.

"I have an important note for you from Mr Rorke. I can't bring it down because I'm on duty. Please come up and get it."

Intrigued, Nancy replied, "Okay."

As she quickly put on slacks and sweater, Nancy kept wondering what the note might say. Was it a further confession, a clue to the treasure, or perhaps a warning?

Bess and George had not awakened and she did not disturb them. Nancy hurried up the corridor and climbed the metal stairway to the open area above. The sailor was working at one of the big lifeboats on deck near the prow. He was untying the heavy canvas tarpaulin stretched over it under the direction of a heavy-set crewman. Together they laid the canvas on deck.

"Good morning, miss," the sailor said. "This guy's got a note." He walked off and disappeared.

Nancy went up to the burly crewman. "You have a note for me from Mr Rorke?"

"It's a message," the man replied. "He says to tell you you're goin' t' be punished for not mindin' your own business, Miss Nancy Drew!"

In a surprise move the sailor knocked Nancy down so that she sprawled on top of the tarpaulin. Before she could get up, he had pulled the canvas round her and now tied the ropes tightly.

"Help! Help!" Nancy cried, but the sounds were too muffled for anyone to hear.

Seconds later she felt herself being lifted up and then thrown. She landed in the water and began to sink!

The End of the Quest

NED Nickerson's cabin was next to the one Nancy, Bess, and George occupied. He had also heard Nancy's name spoken, and the summons for her to come up on deck. At first he had thought little of it, but upon second thoughts it worried him.

Leaning out his porthole, he called to Nancy but there was no response. Alarmed now, Ned threw on some clothes and dashed up to the deck above. From a distance he could see Nancy being rolled into the tarpaulin and quickly tied up. Ned dashed forward but he was too late to keep the burly seaman from hurling her overboard!

"You rat!" he yelled at the man.

With a tremendous swing at the sailor's jaw he sent him crashing to the deck in a knockout punch. The next second Ned was poised on the rail, then he dived into the water.

Nancy was not in sight. Because of the weight of the tarpaulin she had plummeted straight down. There was enough air inside it to breathe for a few minutes and Nancy struggled hard to free herself. But her attempts were futile. She knew now that she would die of suffocation rather than drown.

"Poor Dad!" Nancy thought. "And I promised him

I'd be careful." Then she added, "I don't want to leave Ned and Bess and George and Hannah, too—all the people I love!"

Suddenly Nancy became aware of something touching her. Within seconds the rope was untied and the tarpaulin was being unrolled. Then, as if a miracle had happened, she was free! Nancy was already holding her breath, and with help from Ned, she swam to the surface.

By this time Bess, George, Dave, and Burt had been awakened by the young sailor. Having thought over the episode of the note, he had begun to suspect trouble. The young people had rushed to the deck and were puzzled to find the crewman unconscious.

Just then two heads broke the surface of the water. The onlookers were aghast to see Nancy and Ned, now taking in great gulps of fresh air.

"They have on ordinary clothes," Bess commented. "What's happened?"

Burt leaned over the rail. "Need a hand?" he called.

"Guess we can make it," Ned called back. "Get the captain. And put down the ladder."

Dave dashed off. When Captain Stryver arrived, the two bedraggled swimmers were back on deck. Nancy and Ned told what had happened and pointed to the burly seaman, who was just reviving.

The captain yanked the sailor, John Todd, to his feet and demanded an explanation. He said that Rorke had told him when he reached New York he was to go to a certain place and receive a large amount of money for "putting Nancy Drew out of the picture."

Under his breath Burt said, "And he's too dumb to know he'd be double-crossed and never get a cent."

Todd said the young sailor was innocent. He had been asked to summon Nancy because she knew him. He apologized profusely to Nancy and to the captain.

"Nancy," said George, as Todd was taken away, "you're shivering. Let's go and get some dry clothes."

"And a hot breakfast," Bess added.

Half an hour later everyone gathered in the captain's dining-room. In order not to alarm Trixie, Nancy had requested that no mention be made of what had happened. Conversation was all about the hunt for the treasure.

"I want to dig," said Trixie. She reached under the table and brought out a small pail with a shovel. She kept looking into it and smiling. "I got a map," she said.

"May I see it?" Nancy asked.

"I don't want to show it," Trixie replied.

"Why not?" her mother asked. "And where did you get it?"

Trixie's lips began to quiver. On the verge of tears she answered, "From a drawer in Nancy's cabin."

Mrs Chatham scolded her daughter. When the girl began to cry, Mr Smith tried to quieten her by showing his copy of half the old map.

Nancy spoke up. "Don't worry. Trixie, you never could have found the treasure with that half map, even if it had been matched with the good half."

"What do you mean?" the little girl asked.

As everyone listened in amazement, Nancy explained. "When Irene and Fred Brown followed me that day and I was afraid they might steal the exact copy of Mr Smith's map, I posted it to Dad at his office. However, before I did, I made another drawing of it, but I deliberately reversed all the directions. And that's the paper you have, Trixie."

Everyone laughed and George said, "Leave it to Nancy to outwit the schemers!"

The Smiths were eager to start the treasure hunt. Ellen's father felt much better and insisted upon going. Digging tools were procured and the group set off in rowing-boats.

When they assembled on the beach of Little Palm Island, Nancy rearranged her figures on the half map to give the correct directions. Then work started near a large palm tree. Soon mound after mound of sandy soil had been turned up. No treasure chest was revealed.

A disheartening thought struck Nancy. Suppose the treasure had been dug up long ago and carried away!

She went off by herself, and using a compass, refigured the directions. "What a goose I've been!" she scolded herself as she looked at the result. "We've been working at the wrong spot!"

She hurried back to tell the others and chose a different palm tree for the search. It stood on a beautiful knoll overlooking the rolling sea.

"I'm sure this is the place!" Nancy exclaimed, marking off a large rectangle on the ground.

Again the young people turned up the sandy soil and loose rocks. After fifteen minutes Ned's spade struck a hard object.

"Probably just a rock," he said, without much hope.

Turning up another spadeful of earth he bent to examine the object.

"This is no rock!" he shouted jubilantly. "I think we've found the treasure!"

The other boys rushed to help him dig. Presently

the top of a rusty iron chest was uncovered. In another five minutes they were able to lift it from the hole.

"This seems too good to be true," Ellen said, tears of happiness in her eyes.

"Nancy," Mr Smith spoke up, "you must have the honour of opening the lid."

"If you don't mind," she answered, "I'd rather you three Smiths do it. But the chest must be prised open with a crowbar."

Ned offered to do this and soon succeeded. As Mr Smith raised the lid, everyone stared in stunned silence. Inside lay hundreds of gold and silver coins, jewellery and rich ornaments from all over the world. That the wealth had been the property of Ellen's great-grand-father, Captain Tomlin, there could be no doubt, for a stained letter addressed to his descendants bore his signature.

Mrs Smith clasped her husband's hands in happiness, and Ellen exclaimed, "Dad! Everything's going to be fine from now on!"

Congratulations, handshakes, and thanks were ex-changed. Everyone praised Nancy, who modestly reminded them, "Without Mrs Chatham we couldn't have made the trip."

The Smiths, Bill Tomlin, and Mrs Chatham con-sulted together, with the result that they presented a generous gift to the Heyborns, and similar tokens for every member of the expedition. Nancy received a beautiful jewelled bracelet, one of the finest pieces in the collection.

The chest was prepared for transfer to the *Primrose*. With such a precious cargo aboard, Captain Stryver was worried that the prisoners might get loose and make trouble. He tried to keep the news from them, but they overheard the excited conversations of the others. The three captives were furious, each blaming the other for their failure to obtain the treasure. Before the voyage home was begun, however, a government seaplane arrived and to everyone's relief took charge of the captives.

"How did the men get together in the first place?" the young people asked Nancy, who had been present when the prisoners confessed.

"When Rorke failed to buy Mr Smith's half of the map, he got in touch with his old friend Spike," she explained. "To his surprise he found his partner had also heard the story from the *Warwick's* first mate, and was working on it from the Captain John Tomlin angle."

As Nancy paused, George spoke up. "When Spike traced Mrs Chatham, it was easy for him to snoop around Rocky Edge. He knew the place because years before he had robbed it."

"Spike hid in the house and in the studio," Nancy continued. "He overheard many things, and learned that Mrs Chatham had a lot of money in a safe. When he needed some cash, he decided to kidnap Trixie for a sizeable ransom."

George spoke up again. "But Nancy found her in time."

"The messenger was to be Snorky, but he saw us leaving the studio and cut out quickly," Nancy put in. "Incidentally, he did steer the *Primrose* off course on purpose."

She went on, "Spike used the secret room in the studio to examine all the papers he could lay his hands on. When Trixie and I kept showing up, he tried to scare us away."

"Did he admit to stealing my half of the map?" Ellen's father asked.

"Yes. Rorke got him to do that. The arresting officers have it now."

"Where do the Browns fit in?" Bill Tomlin inquired.

"They were part of the ring, but didn't get along very well with the others," Nancy explained. "They thought they were smarter than Rorke and Spike. But Spike managed to get the wanted piece of map from them—at least the one Hannah made. She had copied the words 'Little' and 'Pa,' giving him the first word and part of the second in the name of the island, but she had misled him completely in the directions to the buried fortune.

"You know, Hannah Gruen really saved the treasure," Nancy added. "If she had given the right directions in John Tomlin's half of the map to the Browns, the buried chest might have been taken before we reached here!"

"But, Nancy, *you* really solved the mystery!" Ellen exclaimed.

"*Mysteries*, you mean," her father put in warmly. "After all, Nancy traced my brother, the map, the thieves, and the treasure!"

"Oh, please stop it!" Nancy declared, blushing. "I couldn't have done a thing without the help of every one of you, and especially Mrs Chatham for engaging the *Primrose*."

"Nonsense!" the woman replied. "This trip did more for me and Trixie than you'll ever know."

Nancy was happy about this, but at once began to long for another mystery.

That evening when she and Ned were on deck gazing at the moon, he said, "Nancy, how about taking your mind of mysteries for a while and thinking of me instead?"

Nancy laughed mischievously. She gave a mock salute and said, "Aye, aye, sir!"